HIS HAT WAS SUDDENLY TORN FROM HIS HEAD AS HE HEARD THE CRACK OF A RIFLE...

Slocum slammed his heels into the horse's sides, crouching low over the animal's neck as it charged into a gallop. At the same instant he was already slipping the Winchester out of the saddle scabbard under his left leg; working the action single-handed. Two more bullets scorched within inches of his head.

In that desperate moment he was figuring that whoever was shooting at him didn't know his job very well; for after missing the first shot the bushwhacker should have gone for the horse. Once the animal was down, with its rider afoot, the killer could have taken his time picking him off. Instead he made the dumb choice of trying to blast his man out of the saddle.... Just then Slocum spotted the spurt of dust a couple of yards ahead of the pony's forefeet and he knew the man had decided to go for the animal.

OTHER BOOKS BY JAKE LOGAN

JAKE LOGAN

BLOOD AT
THE CROSSING

BERKLEY BOOKS, NEW YORK

BLOOD AT THE CROSSING

A Berkley Book / published by arrangement with
the author

PRINTING HISTORY
Berkley edition / September 1988

ISBN: 0-425-11233-0

A BERKLEY BOOK ® 757,375
Berkley Books are published by The Berkley Publishing Group,
200 Madison Avenue, New York, N.Y. 10016.
The name "BERKLEY" and the "B" logo
are trademarks belonging to Berkley Publishing Corporation.

PRINTED IN THE UNITED STATES OF AMERICA

10 9 8 7 6 5 4 3 2 1

1

It was a long trail to Hardins Crossing; south and east from Butte. But John Slocum was in no hurry. He was enjoying the ride through the high country. The trail was new to him, and he could see it hadn't been traveled in some while. Rocky, narrow, overgrown with brush, hazardous with fallen timber; there were even places where the trail had washed out and he'd had to dismount and lead the little spotted pony. He wasn't all that familiar with this part of the country southeast of Butte, northwest of the Yellowstone, and all he could do was simply follow the trail toward Horse Gap.

At Horse Gap he'd still be in the high country, with rugged going ahead, and so he'd simply make his way in the general direction of Hardins Crossing; a place he'd never seen. He was figuring it would be best if he didn't ride openly along the regular trails. His departure from

Butte, in the western Montana Territory, hadn't been exactly a celebration.

All the same, he was getting closer to Horse Gap, and now, breaking out of the tough trail he'd been traveling for about three hours, he struck a narrow game track heading almost directly toward the Yellowstone and soon found himself circling around a high benchland. It occurred to him that he could go up and over the bench, but he quickly reasoned that he would be exposed—always a mistake for a man in new country.

Now drawing rein, he sat the chunky spotted pony, a horse that had stood him in good stead since he'd broken him two years ago over on the Musselshell. He waited, his clear, cat-green eyes feeling over the land. And he listened, letting his eyes soften in order to be more acute to his surroundings. Now he caught the flash of a coyote streaking for cover far down the trail. Looking down near his horse's feet he spotted day-old deer tracks. But still there was no sign of horse or of human, red or white.

He knew he wasn't far from Crow country. It had been a while ago that he'd trapped on the other side of those rimrocks—mink, martin, muskrat had been abundant, though by that time the mountain men had trapped out all the beaver. He sat the horse, absolutely still now, wholly alert, yet open and loose.

There was something; he wasn't satisfied. Only what? The tribes and whites were at peace, but that was a fragile situation at best. Something had tightened in him, a signal that he had learned early in his years to take as a warning.

Presently, and for no obvious reason at all, he shifted his weight, laying one of the reins across his pony's neck to move him gently. And it was that little step taken by the horse that saved his life. His hat was suddenly torn from his head as he heard the crack of the rifle, and he slammed his heels into the horse's sides, crouching low over the animal's neck as it charged into a gallop. At the same instant he was already slipping the Winchester out of the saddle scabbard under his left leg, working the action single-handed. Two more bullets scorched within inches of his head.

In that desperate moment he was figuring that whoever was shooting at him didn't know his job very well, for after missing the first shot the bushwhacker should have gone for the horse. Once the animal was down, with its rider afoot, the would-be killer could have simply taken his time picking him off. Instead he made the dumb choice of trying to blast his man out of the saddle, evidently not understanding how hard it was to hit a weaving man on a racing horse. But just then Slocum spotted the spurt of dust a couple of yards ahead of his pony's forefeet, and he knew the man had decided to go for the animal.

Hauling back on the reins with all his weight, he pulled his horse to a hard stop, throwing up a sheet of dust. He threw himself out of the saddle, landing hard on the hard ground, and immediately righted himself and was dragging the animal behind some rocks. The would-be killer had been caught by surprise, and his next shot didn't even come close.

By now, Slocum had caught the powder smoke up on the rocky rim. He lifted the Winchester and aimed swiftly as his keen eyes caught the flash of a blue shirt. Squeezing off two rounds, he ducked and, bent over, ran a half-dozen yards to a new spot, still covered by the rocks, then leapt down through an opening onto a flat ledge and rolled in tight against the high bank of earth and rock that reared up behind him.

He didn't think he had hit his man, at least not seriously, for immediately three shots raked close to him and he crouched even lower, making himself as small as he could while the bullets spanged off rock and whined into the hot blue sky.

By his count the bushwhacker's rifle ought now to be empty, and while the man reloaded was the time to move closer for a clean shot.

But the bushwhacker, though he hadn't used his head in missing his chance to shoot the spotted horse early on, turned out not to be all that green. He clearly figured that Slocum would take advantage of the gap in the shooting and try to move in closer, so when his target now ran along the ledge in a crouch, he pumped off two shots, and Slocum, hit in the shoulder, slammed against one of the big rocks.

He slid down to his knees, and a third, whining bullet cut a groove in the rock close to his head. He let his breath out fast, for that had been close enough to really tighten him. Damn! Yet he had to give the man credit. The bushwhacker had simply dropped his rifle and, instead of reloading as Slocum had thought he would do, was using a second gun, catching his quarry out in the open. Slocum realized now that it was his memory of the gunman's mistake in not shooting his horse that had led him to take the man for an inexperienced killer. He'd been lucky!

He figured that the man trying to kill him had to know he'd been hit, though he likely couldn't see him. Quickly he examined his wound as best he could, without moving from his position, which at least for the moment was safe. The bullet had only cut a shallow groove across his left shoulder. It was bleeding, however. He wrapped his bandanna around the wound, tying it one-handed.

"Slocum! Yer done for, goddamn you!"

Right on top of those words came a tremendous explosion as a charge of buckshot tore across the rocks directly above his head, spraying him with rock dust.

The gunman had a cut-down shotgun in use, and Slocum knew he had to be really close and in a deadly position to use it like that. Slocum knew his position was too vulnerable for him to wait. He had to do something fast.

Dropping the Winchester and pulling up his legs for leverage, he suddenly hurled himself clear of the rocks, knowing the terrible chance he was taking. At the same instant he drew his Colt, and, twisting his body, ignoring the pain in his shoulder, his eyes swept the terrain for sign of his attacker.

The man was on a ledge barely fifteen feet away, and the twin barrels of that deadly shotgun were right on Slocum while he was still in his desperate dive.

He had aimed for a patch of sand, and as his body struck it, his left hand slapped down on the hammer spur of the Colt, which he was holding in his right.

He lay still, watching the man shudder as the lead found its target and the shotgun went off wildly, bucking out of his hands. He was a big man, and he staggered with little steps along the ledge, quite out of control of himself as a sort of death dance took over, and then he tumbled down to the dry, dusty trail. He landed in the rocks and sage, and the thud of his big, heavy body said it all. There was no need for Slocum to go down there.

Yet, after waiting a long moment, he climbed down and turned the body over and looked down into the face of the man who had failed to kill him. It was a man he had never seen before. A search through his pockets told him nothing. The man was—nobody. He had come from nowhere, and God knows where he was now. He had called Slocum's name, and so he had known who he was. Evidently a paid killer, Slocum decided. Well, he sure wouldn't be spending that money in a hurry. But why? Who wanted to kill him that badly?

And yet later, looking back over it, he realized that even as he stood looking down at the dead man something in him knew it wasn't over. In that moment something in him knew the truth, and he remembered the trick with the second gun. Just in time he dropped and rolled as the shot cracked down into the little draw, slapping past his head. But he was firing at the flash as he fell, and he heard the cry of pain and surprise as the man crouching up on the high rock stretched straight up from the force of the bullet that killed him and, without even a sigh or a whisper, tumbled down to lie right on top of the first bushwhacker as Slocum dove for cover.

This time it was indeed over. Slocum waited a long time, just to be really sure. He waited, feeling the atmosphere all around him, breathing gently himself, but without making a sound.

Finally, he stood up, walked over and checked the second body. There was still no identity. For a moment he wondered why the second man had waited so long to take a shot at him; then he saw that he'd been wounded before receiving the final bullet. It must have been a bad one, for not only was his shirt soaked with blood but so were his trousers. Slocum figured his final bullet from the Winchester had hit him in the guts, while it looked like his earlier shot had torn open his chest and part of his neck. The man must have known he was done for when he made that last effort to succeed where his partner had failed. Slocum noticed that he was young; he might have put it that he was a boy. It gave him an odd feeling that somebody so young would want to kill him.

He stood there for a few moments, piecing the battle together. Two of them. Somebody had really wanted to make sure. Somebody who respected his ability. And it was definitely not the law. Who then? Surely someone who'd been expecting him to travel this way, someone who had known he was heading for Hardins Crossing.

He moved into the shade of some aspen now and checked his shoulder, then, still satisfied that it wasn't really bad, he carefully replaced the bandanna.

Suddenly he heard something in the stand of aspen just in front of him and his hand swept to his gun, but it was the spotted horse. He'd been hit in the leg and was lying down, thrashing every once in a while and now letting out a whinny of fear and pain.

The only thing Slocum could do was shoot him. That left him afoot and a good distance from where he was heading. He stripped the dead animal. It wasn't easy getting his stock saddle off, with the horse lying on it, but he managed, though it didn't help his shoulder any.

He found the horses of the two men who had tried to kill him without any difficulty. In that clear, high air it was easy enough to smell them. He stripped the smaller animal of the two, a bay, and threw on his own rigging. Slocum could see the bay would do well in the high altitude—better than the sorrel, who was narrow-chested and seemed to be favoring his left forefoot. Neither mount was as good as the spotted pony, and it was clear to him that their riders hadn't known much about horseflesh, or at any rate hadn't cared. Both horses carried the same shoulder brand, a circle slash. Of course the bushwhackers could have rented their mounts, which also might have accounted for their poor condition. Both needed their hooves trimmed.

It was getting toward mid-afternoon when he finally mounted up. The sun was beating across the sky, drawing little beads of sweat on his face, the back of his neck, and on the backs of his hands.

He knew the would-be killers hadn't been trailing him, and so they had somehow known he was headed toward Horse Gap, and possibly Hardins Crossing, and had set up an ambush. That meant there could be some habitation not very far away. A ranch maybe, though it wouldn't be a big spread this high up. Or it could be a line camp.

Along about sundown, when he'd been riding for maybe three hours he came upon the wagon tracks. The trail had dropped down swiftly, and he was in the valley through which ran the Horse Gap River. He recognized it right off, and then it came back to him as he studied the wagon tracks that he'd heard Horse Gap was now a stage depot. He'd forgotten that over the years the settlement of a couple of log cabins had turned into a part of a stage route where horses were changed and passengers could rest.

The light was going swiftly out of the sky now, and so he decided not to ride in but to wait till morning, when he would walk in with his saddle rigging and warbag. It wouldn't do to be riding a horse with a brand he knew nothing about.

He made a dry camp, ate beef jerky and some soda biscuits, then lay down on his bedroll, fully clothed, with his guns close. He had turned the sorrel pony loose, figuring it would find its way back to where it'd come from. In the morning he would do the same with the bay, just outside Horse Gap, and he'd take the stage into Hardins Crossing. It was of course asking for trouble to be without a horse in this country. No wonder they hanged horse thieves, he reflected ruefully.

Just before he dropped off to a very light sleep he wondered again if the two bushwhackers had anything to do with his going to Hardins Crossing to meet Big Ben McCormack.

He heard a coyote barking nearby, and he heard the

jingle of the bay horse's bridle as he chomped on the tight buffalo grass. And then he slept. He slept as he always did on the trail—just beneath the surface, half asleep and half awake.

2

Slocum hunkered back into the corner of the stagecoach, his hat pulled down over his eyes, though not letting the brim cut off his vision. He had been feigning sleep, studying his fellow passengers, the two men and the blond girl. They'd arrived on the stage at Horse Gap, where the driver had changed horses; and now they were only about twenty minutes gone from the depot when there came the rifle shot and the shouted command to pull up.

Slocum had his eyes on the girl as they came to a racking stop and dust billowed in through the half-open window. With a motion that was almost a sleight of hand it was so fast, the girl with the corn-yellow hair drew a long pin from her bonnet, hitched up her voluminous skirt, and pinned her purse to her undergarments.

Slocum swiftly noted the handsome shaft of leg that appeared, and he observed too how the two male passengers took note of the occasion. He almost grinned; even in the face of danger a shapely leg, an appealing bosom had to be honored.

One of the men had pulled a gun from inside his coat. He was a foolish-looking young man, and his gun was an equally foolish little derringer. For it was obvious from the sounds outside the stagecoach that there were a number of holdup men, and clearly well armed.

"Put that thing on the floor!" the girl said sharply. "You aimin' to get us all killed?"

"But, miss, uh, ma'am . . ."

"On the floor!" the girl snapped. "And give 'em your money nice and polite when they ask for it."

Slocum figured from the sound outside that there had to be at least three men. But he remained in his corner, hunched, with his hat down.

"Hey, you—you asleep?" the girl said to Slocum.

With his forefinger he casually pushed back the brim of his Stetson and looked openly at her. "Not now, miss."

For a moment she held his glance, not saying anything, and then moved her blue eyes to the window of the coach. They could clearly hear what was being said outside. The man who was talking—obviously one of the holdup party —had a voice like honey on silk—soft, thick, well aware of itself, and enjoying it.

"I'd say Texas," Slocum said, sitting up in his corner and readjusting his hat. "Wouldn't you, miss? Almost sounds too good to be true, don't he."

He watched her eyes taking him in as he reached to his shirt pocket and took out a quirly. As he did so, he also loosened the thong on the Colt .44. The second male passenger—a pink old man with a thick, snow-white mustache that seemed too heavy for his face—was looking at him out of rheumy eyes under which were wide red gutters. His nose was long, thin, and as orange as a carrot.

"I suppose we can expect anything," he said. He sighed all the way through his thin, tube-shaped body, which was firmly wrapped in the tight plaid waistcoat he wore beneath an equally tight black broadcloth coat. "I'll have a story for the papers when we get through this."

"If!" the girl said with sharp emphasis. "Not when— if!"

"Er—yes, quite."

Slocum sat all the way up now; his big, six-foot-plus height and broad shoulders and big hands seemed to crowd the coach. But it was the swift ease of his movement that was impressive even more than his size, or even the sharp green eyes which were accented now by his raven-black hair when he removed his hat and then put it back on again.

"Just pass out your money," said the man at the door of the coach, "and I won't bother you."

He was a sturdy man of average height with a big head. A blue bandanna covered the lower half of his face. The tone of his voice assured Slocum that he was well armed and backed by other guns.

The young man who had put his derringer on the floor handed over a leather purse. Slocum had already put aside some money for the occasion, and he passed it to the man at the coach window.

The masked man looked at it, and Slocum knew he realized it wasn't the whole amount.

"That's it, huh?"

"That's it," Slocum said.

The holdup man's next remark was totally unexpected. "Where'd you pick up the stage?"

"Horse Gap," Slocum said, wondering why he wanted to know. The man could easily have found out from the driver. But he was thinking too of the bay gelding he had left to wander back home with the Circle Slash brand on its shoulder.

"There is a dozen of us," the man with the Texas voice said. "Do not nobody of you fire on us." He said it straight to Slocum, never taking his eyes from the big man's face. And John Slocum knew he had been recognized. It was right then that he began to smell something false about the holdup.

He shifted his weight, but without any obvious motion. It was more of an inner movement.

"Lady?" the masked man said to the girl.

With her blue eyes twinkling, the girl smiled invitingly. Her voice was as soft as velvet. "Honey, why, I purely ain't got a thing."

The road agent removed his hat and bowed his big head, though clumsily. "Why, miss, I would no more think of robbin' a Texas lady than I would think of puttin' a bullet in my own head."

Slocum could hardly restrain his grin of admiration for the scene. At the same time his suspicion of something false about the holdup was growing.

The bandit's eyes swung back to him now. They were no longer smiling, as they had at the girl—they were bone hard over the edge of the blue bandanna. "Don't try to foller, mister."

"I wouldn't think of it," Slocum said in an even voice.

"We unhitched the team, and we'll leave 'em down the road a piece." The bandit's eyes flicked again to the girl.

"I've always admired first-class work," Slocum said with an easy grin as he edged further toward the position he wanted. "But you did forget something."

"Tryin' not to overlook any little thing," the bandit said, and his Texas voice was deeper than ever.

"I didn't hear you order the box thrown down."

When he saw the color rising in the bandit's forehead he knew his wild guess had been right.

"That's right, you didn't," the man at the window said, "but thanks for reminding me." He turned to the girl. "We'll take you with us. So come on." And he started to open the door of the coach.

Slocum moved with the speed of a mountain cat. He had the Colt out and up, pointed right at the bandit's head. "I don't figure you're the kind who wants to die young, mister. So call off your guns out there and ride. You got till I count three."

"I've got rifles trained on you, Slocum."

"And this Colt can bust your head open quicker'n a fly can scratch his ass! I'm counting—one . . ."

"All right, then. For now." And turning his head he called out to his men.

"And leave the money you took."

"We'll meet again, Slocum." The eyes above the bandanna were like hot nails.

"I'll look forward to it," Slocum said. "Now you tell them to ride off without you. And call the driver over, so he can tell me you're not trying to pull anything."

When it had been done, and he heard the horses pounding away, he pushed open the door of the coach. "Let's take a look at you." And with his left hand he reached out and pulled down the bandanna.

The bandit flinched. There was a long scar running down the left side of his face.

"What's your name?"

"Print."

"Print who?"

"Just—Print." And he spat hard on the ground, but

turning his head slightly in order not to hit the man with the gun.

The guard and driver had come up.

"How many riders?" Slocum asked the driver.

"I seen three."

The guard nodded in agreement.

"They'll be waiting for you, Slocum," Print said, and his eyes darted to the girl, who was leaning forward, still inside the coach.

"Get the horses," Slocum said to the driver. Peering out of the coach, yet not taking his eyes away from his prisoner, he saw that the team was close by.

"Where's your horse?" he said to the outlaw.

"Yonder. Not far."

The driver had gone for the team, and now Slocum said to the guard, "Strip his horse and bring the rigging here. We'll take it with us. But take his gunbelt first."

When the guard had the gunbelt, Slocum stepped down from the coach.

"We'd better get out of here," the guard said. "They sure won't go far."

Slocum had climbed up onto the stage and taken his Winchester from his saddle scabbard.

"Take your clothes off," he said to the road agent.

Print's big mouth opened, and so did his little eyes.

"Mister . . ." His eyes went to the girl.

"Be quick about it." Slocum nodded at the girl without looking at her. "You can look away, miss."

"I already am!"

"You're not missing much," Slocum said as Print peeled down to his longhandles. "That'll do 'er," he said then. "Now turn around, hands behind your back. And you tie him," he said to the guard. "Tight. Real tight. You got piggin' string?"

"Sure do, in the boot."

"Do it, then."

"We will get you, Slocum."

"Yeah? You will? Who is 'we'?"

Print said nothing. His jaw was clamped tight when Slocum hit him with his fist. The man staggered and almost fell.

"Tell me!"

It was the pink-faced passenger who spoke now. "Sir, those bandits, those men will surely return, or may even set up an attack farther along the trail."

"We'd better get going," said the other passenger, speaking from a very stiff mouth.

The girl sniffed. She was clearly the calmest of the three passengers. "We better haul it out of here, mister, is what we are all saying. He ain't going to tell you anything, even if you beat him into little pieces. Hell, I know his kind. Texas tough—all the way through."

Slocum knew how right she was. He knew the kind of man he was dealing with. He knew too that he *could* beat it out of him, but they didn't have the time.

By now the driver had hitched his team and the driver had swung up onto the box.

The guard canted his head at Slocum. He was a tough old bird with bandy legs and big knuckles on his hands. "You still want him tied, do you?"

"Behind his back." He watched while the guard completed the job.

"Who sent you?" Slocum said, taking a last try. "And who were those two who tried to drygulch me north of Horse Gap?"

But Print's silence was as firm as death.

Slocum took a quick look around and then swung into the coach. His last view of the bandit was his furious red face disappearing in a cloud of dust as he stood in his longhandles, stolid as a scaffold. There was no need to wonder what he was feeling.

"Jesus!" the girl said as she rocked back into her seat. "You nigh got the whole bunch of us killed."

"Nigh is still a miss, honey," Slocum said with a grin.

"How did you know that feller wouldn't shoot you?" she asked. "I mean, when you first braced him. He could have."

"Because he wanted you alive."

"But how did you know that?" the thin young man asked. He had taken off his brown derby hat and now ran the palm of his hand over his slick, pomaded brown hair. He was clean-shaven save for tidy sideburns and a trim little mustache. But he was still obviously excited from the encounter with Print and his boys.

"It was easy to see he wasn't robbing the stage or he would have ordered down the box. So it had to be— what?" He looked at the girl. "You. He started to take you with him."

"I never saw him before in my life!"

"I'm not saying you did. But he was mighty surprised to see me. This threw him off. Guess he knew my face from somewhere."

"I don't get it," the girl said, and released a long sigh. "There've been stage holdups nearly every day—and here, this time they don't even want the express box."

"I think you do get it," Slocum said. "They were after you, not out to rob the coach, though they weren't against picking up a little extra boodle." He looked at her carefully then as he said, "So who were they, really? And why were they after you?"

She leaned forward, her hands wide apart in an offering

gesture. "Search me, mister. I don't know them any more than you do."

"You don't know of anyone had it in for you? Would want to capture you, maybe do you harm?"

"I do not—and that's the God's truth!" There were two tears, one for each eye. And Slocum wasn't so sure she wasn't telling the truth.

"What's your name?" he asked.

"Mellody. Honey Mellody—spelled with two l's, is how my old man always used to say it," she added, recovering some of her bright spirits.

"Is it really spelled with two l's?" the thin man in the brown derby asked. "I've always spelled 'Melody' with one." As he finished speaking he reached up with both hands and adjusted his hat, touching the brim with extreme care.

"I dunno," the girl said. "I never did learn how to spell."

The passenger with the pink face and snow-white hair now broke his long silence. "By golly, I shall have to get to the tools of my trade. It's a natural—a natural story of the West. The readers back east will devour it!" He beamed at his three companions. "Oh, pardon me, I should introduce myself. I am, as you've possibly surmised, a writer. T. Wellington Throneberry is the name, often referred to as T.W. You may call me the same. If you wish," he added. "If you wish." He leveled his glassy blue eyes at Slocum. "Quaint sort of holdup, uh—as you in fact put it yourself. Eh?"

Slocum said nothing.

"I believe that man appeared to recognize you, sir. Might I ask your name? Of course, I can change it in my story." He coughed gently into his loosely clenched fist at that point, and sniffed.

Slocum's face and voice were equally straight as he said, "My name is George Washington."

The young man under the brown derby checked a furious grin at that but managed to control his face; the girl burst into a raucous laugh, slapping her hand against her thigh; while T. Wellington Throneberry rose to the occasion with superb ease. "I am delighted to meet you, Mr. Washington. Might I ask—do you happen to be a direct or an indirect descendant of our first president?"

"I wouldn't want to lie to you," Slocum said. And he realized he was in the presence of an individual who might or might not have been a real writer, but the man sitting opposite him in the bouncing coach was without question a con man of unusual, not to say first-class, talent.

Slocum leaned out the window, taking a look at the sky and where the sun stood. Lifting his voice to reach above the clatter of the running horses and the creaking coach, he called out to the men on the box, "Any sign of those riders?"

"Nope!"

"Good enough! Whip 'em, driver. We want to see Hardins Crossing sooner than soon!"

Hardins Crossing lay in the socket of a long valley. High mountains to the west brought early evening and nightfall to the town. There was timber to the north, running into the foothills of the mountains, while the east and south were an endless vista of prairie. In the valley the feed was good and cattle grazed. Hardins was cattle country. Not so long ago it had been famous for its mines. But the mines had flooded and the town had gone bust. Driven to the extremity of becoming another ghost town, Hardins Crossing had suddenly attracted the cattle trade. Ranchers found the grass plentiful; and as a handy way-stop on the trail to

Milton, the shipping point for the southern herds, Hardins began to revive. And then, to everyone's surprise, the largest and most profitable mine was drained of its water and was back in operation.

A town of some thousand citizens, Hardins—as it was more popularly called—supported all the necessaries—a livery, a general store, three eateries, a couple of rooming houses, and an amiable number of saloons, gaming establishments, and cribs, with friendly partners for frolic. There was a school, a church, both with suitable personnel, and a cemetery. There was a lawyer, a doctor, an undertaker. There was also a newspaper, the *Hardins Settler.*

At each end of Main Street a sign was posted stating that no animals were allowed to graze in the roadway, there would be no racing of horses, and visitors would leave their firearms with the sheriff until their departure from town. Both notices had been printed freehand and were punctuated liberally with bullet holes.

The majority of the houses were wood; some were logs, others framed. A short distance from the north end of town stood a two-story brick house, and there were some two-story wooden structures along Main Street.

The stage depot was a log building at the east end of the town, and now, as the stage from Horse Gap drove in, the team at a walk, none of the three or four loungers inhabiting the obviously newly built porch seemed the least bit interested. However, when the driver and guard alighted with news of the holdup, and the peculiar fact that the money box was untouched, interest and shortly high curiosity took over, even driving one oldster from his chair to spit over the edge of the porch.

Slocum didn't waste any time. Nodding goodbye to the girl and the two men, he hefted his warbag and saddle rig and made for the livery, which one of the hangers-on pointed out to him. Even the warmth of Honey Mellody's farewell look didn't deter him. He was pretty sure he could find her if he wanted to. He was pretty sure, too, that he'd be hearing from whoever had ordered the fake stage robbery, not to mention the failed bushwhacking.

At the livery he deposited his saddle gear with the hostler, asked directions to a rooming house or hotel and a barber-bath, and then looked at the horses.

"Might take a look at that bay horse there," he said to the hostler, a cavernous individual with no more than two upper and three lower front teeth.

"See you know horseflesh," the oldster said, wrinkles suddenly filling his long, high forehead as he surveyed the bay horse. "You buyin' or leasin'?"

"Like to handle him some," Slocum said as he walked over and, laying his hand on the bay's left shoulder, looked down at his foot. "Does he favor that foot? I had a notion when you walked him out."

"You got a sharp eye, mister."

"I know. But how about answering my question?"

"He does. But he's gettin' over it."

Slocum's big hand slid down the bay's leg, and he lifted the hoof to look at it. "Looks to be a sore frog there," he said, pushing with his thumb.

The hostler sniffed. He had a very long nose, which added to his gaunt look.

"Well, I ain't got time now, I'll come back," Slocum said to him. "But dig me up something I can ride. I reckon you've figured by now you can't cheat me."

And he turned abruptly and walked off, carrying his warbag. His shoulder was hurting, and so he decided he'd stop at the doc and see about some salve.

He had just put his hand on the doorknob over which the large sign read DOCTOR when the soft, musical voice behind him said, "I'm afraid Dr. Barney is indisposed. He won't be in today, sir."

Slocum turned to face the girl in the light gray riding habit. She was young, not much over twenty, with jet-black hair and china-blue eyes. The eyes, the soft, wide mouth, indeed her whole face was smiling pleasantly at him. "Can I help you in any way? I'm Jilly Barney."

Slocum's finger touched the brim of his hat as he shifted his stance. "I dunno, ma'am, or miss."

"Miss."

"I wanted to get some salve for my shoulder. Got creased by a Winchester a while back. Just thought some salve might ease it a bit."

She had opened the door and now walked into the office, bidding him to follow. "Let's take a look," she said.

"Ma'am?"

"Besides being Dr. Barney's daughter, I am also a medical student—of sorts, I suppose. Anyhow, I assist him." She pointed to his left shoulder. "Left one, that it?"

"How'd you guess?" he said, dropping his warbag on the floor.

She didn't answer, but smiled as he unbuttoned his shirt. "Better sit down here."

Her hands were quick, soft, and he could tell she knew what she was doing as she undid the bandanna and inspected his wound.

"Not bad. I'll wash it and dress it, and you'll be as good as new."

"I'm about that already," Slocum said, his eyes following her buttocks across the room to the medicine cabinet that was standing against the wall.

"This ought to fix you up," she said, looking at the label of the jar she was carrying as she returned to him. "It's supposed to be especially good for horses, by the way."

"Then it's for me."

They both laughed at that, and as she bent toward his shoulder, he caught the fragrance of her. At the same time, the nearness of her breasts pushing against her silk blouse brought his organ to full rigidity so that he had to shift in his seat.

"Did it hurt?" she asked. "I was trying to be gentle."

"Oh no, it's fine."

"This'll do you," she said finally, and she stepped back.

"When should I come again?" he asked.

"You don't need to, unless it hurts badly. It'll be stiff. Leave it like that for a couple of days, then check it. Maybe you'd better come in and see Dad, as a matter of fact."

"I'd rather come and see you," Slocum said.

She was standing before him, her hands together at her waist, with a pensive look on her face as she drew in her lower lip. "I see."

"I don't know how you see," Slocum said with a smile. "But you sure look terrific."

At that she burst out laughing, and he thought his erection would burst his trousers. Her laugh ran all the way through him.

Then she said, "Come and see the doctor in a couple of days, just to make sure."

"And when can I see you?"

"I'm afraid you'll have to ask my husband the answer to that, sir."

His eyes had instantly dropped to her hand, which she now held up.

"No, I don't have a ring. You see, I'm getting married tomorrow."

Slocum stood up, lifting his warbag as he did so. "That's a pity, miss. Anyhow, good luck to you."

And suddenly her face was blank, her eyes tight. "Thank you. Good day, sir. And good luck to you."

He felt she had indeed gone suddenly dull as he stepped outside onto the boardwalk and heard the door close quietly behind him.

He was all the way up to the other end of the street, almost at the hotel the hostler had recommended when he realized that he hadn't offered to pay for the salve and bandaging. Good enough. He'd have a good reason for going back later.

3

Deputy Sheriff Hobe Winchy thoughtfully fingered his stubbled jowls and squinted through the dust-smeared window of the sheriff's office. He reached out and rubbed the glass again to make the view clearer. And now he had a pretty good look at the tall stranger who had crossed Main Street right in front of an oncoming freighter's wagon and had stepped up onto the wooden boardwalk and was now pushing through the batwing doors of the Only Chance Saloon.

Hobe Winchy happened to be a deputy more by necessity than intent. Sheriff Swede Byrner, having received more than an ample dose of lead in a brisk gunfight with some Saturday-night roisterers, was still recovering from the encounter. Meanwhile the law in Hardins Crossing had to be maintained; and Hobe, being the only person available, was chosen by Swede, and the town council had agreed.

Hobe was a young man with a thicket of bright red hair, one walleye, which made it difficult for an adversary to tell where he was looking, and a lot of muscle. He had prominent elbows and knees which he used to good advantage when necessary. At the moment Hobe's flaming red hair was hardly visible save for his long sideburns, due to the fact that he was wearing his sweat-stained Stetson hat. As always.

Hobe, while being Swede Byrner's choice only because there was nobody else, for his part had dreamed of being a lawman since he was a shaver. Mostly, Hobe had the reputation of hanging around. He'd been in a number of scrapes, was quick with gun, temper, fists. Swede Byrner, a man in his sixties, had argued the council with the view that Hobe could learn, and that he had all the physical attributes necessary for the job. The council had demurred, but their decision was made when Swede got shot up, and quite by chance Hobe had been on the spot to help out. Those villains were now paying for their crimes by suffering "eternal damnation" in the town's Boot Hill—or, as some of the ruder little boys who scamped around the town put it, the Bone Orchard, courtesy of Hardins' now heavily wounded sheriff.

Hobe didn't give a damn what people thought; or so he was fond of telling himself, like many a town tough. Reflecting on this characteristic as he stood at the window, he suddenly thought of his dead father, then Swede Byrner's daughter, and finally Jilly Barney. But all at once something drove this last pleasing daydream from his mind. For he realized who that stranger going into the Only Chance might be.

Quickly he turned back to Swede Byrner's desk and

found the wanted dodger that had come just the other day. He stood looking down at the picture for a long moment, and at last a grin took over his mouth, and he squinted through his good eye, first at the picture and then at the gun cabinet on the other side of the small room.

"Got him right off, by God!" he said aloud, and he folded the dodger and put it into his hip pocket. Then he crossed to the little table with the washbowl and pitcher on it and looked into the piece of broken mirror that was nailed to the wall. Stepping back a little to get the right view, he looked to see if his tarnished brass star was firmly attached to his shirt, and in the right position. The mirror was too small for him to see his whole reflection, but he imagined how he looked, and he looked good. He checked his sidearm, lifting it out of its holster and dropping it back in. Then he tried a couple of practice draws. Yes, he was loose. He would have to be. And that was all to the good, for he could use the reputation such a killing would bring. In fact, he was thinking as he adjusted his hat, he'd really be on top of it all. But he would be careful, too. He would see how the play went and not rush anything.

As he strode across the street to the Only Chance he was whistling softly under his breath, and when he saw two of his drinking pals entering just ahead of him he nodded knowingly to them and pointed his thumb in the direction of the man who had just entered. As he moved past them to enter the saloon first he said softly, "You boys split inside and cover my play." Hobe Winchy was bursting with readiness as he let the batwings slap together behind him. His sudden good fortune was all but overwhelming him.

Slocum spotted the deputy in the big mirror in back of the bar the moment he entered the saloon. He had ordered a beer and was leaning easily on the mahogany as the lawman drew up beside him. Then he saw the two other men come in. He knew the type well, and when he saw one of them throw a quick look at where he and the lawman were standing he knew there was going to be trouble.

The bartender poured one for Hobe while Slocum watched in the mirror. Hobe had a space between his front teeth, and sometimes his speech would be accompanied by whistling. This was one of those times as he half turned his head toward the man next to him.

"I'm sheriff here in Swede Byrner's absence. Hobe Winchy's the name. Sheriff Hobe Winchy. I make it a rule to say how-de-do to strangers passin' through." He paused, downed his shot glass of whiskey, sighed wetly, and waited for a response.

There was none forthcoming. Slocum simply continued looking into the big mirror, which showed him almost the entire room.

"We don't welcome drifters in Hardins," the deputy went on. "See, I like for a man to get the straight of things right off from the start."

"Where's the real sheriff?" Slocum said coldly, without turning to the man beside him.

"Shot up. I am handling things meanstwhile." Hobe did not like the way the talk was going, and so he leaned heavily into his final words.

Slocum was keeping his eyes on the two men he had spotted as following right along with the deputy. Their glances kept coming back to where he was standing alongside the other man. His position was not good, for with the two at opposite walls and Winchy right beside him, he was caught in a triangle.

Turning now toward the lawman he said, "I appreciate the kindly welcome, Sheriff. I like a man to get things straight too. Like, I am here in this town on my own private business, and I ain't looking for trouble. On the other hand, if trouble comes, I am not a man to be standing around with his hands in his pockets."

His tone had not warmed up. And now he felt rather than saw the deputy's hand drop to his holstered gun.

Hobe Winchy said, "I see you're packing a sidearm, mister. Guns s'posed to be left in the sheriff's office—or on the sober side of the bar, leastways."

"I think that's a good idea," Slocum said, without moving.

Hobe Winchy's breath sounded on a different note now as he sucked it in. "I figger you an' me better have us a little talk, Slocum."

Slocum's face was absolutely blank as he took in the fact that the deputy knew his name. He faced him dead center now, his eyes boring right into the bridge of Hobe Winchy's nose.

The lawman's hand was still on his own gun. And now with his other hand he reached to his back pocket and took out the dodger and dropped it onto the bar. It lay there folded near a small puddle of beer. "That there come in the mail, Slocum. Seems the law still wants you down in Cheyenne."

Slocum ignored the dodger, keeping his eyes on the other man's face. He said nothing, knowing that the deputy had more.

"Big reward for you, Slocum. Don't you want to take a look at that paper there? It says five thousand. That ain't leavin's, mister."

Slocum still remained silent, but now he moved his eyes to the balcony that lined the wall behind the lawman, seeing that it was empty, and then let them drop to the barroom, taking in the two toughs who were obviously ready for action.

"That's a mighty big reward for you, Slocum. It'd sure

be worth a man's while to take you in." He nodded, emphasizing his own words, while his voice lowered, his words barely reaching Slocum.

"You'd have to do it first," Slocum said quietly. "That dodger's a fake. The Cattlemen's Association had 'em printed a good while back, and near drowned the country with them. It don't mean a damn thing."

"Sure, sure." Hobe's grin twisted deeper into his lean face. "Might be a job haulin' you in. Might be considerable. Might even have to whistle up some help. Plenty around, though." He sniffed. "It don't matter actually whether that thing there on the bar be a fake or not. It says what it means—wanted!"

Leaning away from the bar, the deputy bent slightly and spat into a handy though overloaded spittoon. "On the other hand, it might not be such a chore after all. Fact, it could be a question that might even not need to come up."

Slocum's face was still impassive, registering nothing for anyone to see, accompanied by an absolutely neutral tone of voice. "Yeah? How d'you figure?"

Hobe Winchy leaned closer, his free arm touching the edge of the mahogany. "See, the way I sees it, I ought to lock you up and send word down to Cheyenne. But you'd be in the lockup a long while, the mail not being so quick since we got no railroad and only the stage going in that direction."

"I don't believe you heard what I said to you in the first place," Slocum said slowly.

The deputy held up his hand, shaking his head. "I know —I know it's a fake. But see, whoever put that thing out did it for real. See what I mean? See—you're in between the mountain and the gulch, my lad, and whether or not that there dodger's a fake or it ain't don't matter an ounce of cat shit."

Slocum still said nothing, but waited for the lawman to get it all out.

"Now, I, uh, happen to know a man hereabouts is payin' top money for a top gun. Kind of in your line, ain't it? An' I could fix it for you to get to meet him, let us say. Well, I figger that while my duty honor bound is to lock you up, I could be helpin' the situation around about here to relieve the expense of the town holding you in jail all that good while. Say I could get you a job with this man and let's say you could pay me somethin'—like half— what you might figure on, say, you're first month's pay for such a job. Then, see, I could like forget this here." And he tapped the dodger with his middle finger. "Think about it. Think about it. But not too long." And now Hobe's long, black fingernail on his index finger tapped the folded dodger lying on top of the mahogany bar. His walleye seemed to be looking at Slocum.

Slocum had his eyes again on the two men who were siding the deputy. Each had a whiskey and was drinking with his left hand; each also was keeping his eyes carefully away from the tableau at the bar, though not missing a thing.

"What say then, Slocum?" Hobe Winchy was leaning forward, his right hand still on the butt of his Smith & Wesson. "See, even if that dodger was a fake like you say—'ceptin' it isn't—you'd sure have one helluva time tryin' to prove it."

"That's what I know," Slocum said evenly. "I surely do know that, Sheriff."

The grin thickened on Winchy's strange face. "Then you're with me."

"No."

The sheriff straightened up, his smile wiped, his face stiff with anger.

"You can go plumb to hell, mister," Slocum said without a change of tone in his voice, saying it real easy like he was talking about the weather. But now the voice suddenly changed, coming on like a rock. "Beat it!"

In the same instant that he said those words he rammed the whole weight of his big body against the lawman as he felt the man drawing his gun, and at the same time drove his knee right into his crotch.

Hobe Winchy gargled out a sick cry of pain. Slocum grabbed his gun hand and slammed it against the hard bar. The Smith & Wesson dropped to the floor, while its owner sagged in agony from the blow to his groin. Then Slocum hit him right alongside his ear, knocking him to his knees, where he collapsed onto his back on the floor.

But Slocum was not finished. No sooner had he knocked out Winchy—even while the man was still falling—than he had the two men covered with his Colt. And even though they were still at opposite sides of the room, the terrifying speed and power of the big man with the green cat-eyes had registered fully with each. Slocum had them covered even before they'd reached their feet.

"You boys lookin' for trouble, are you?"

Both had dropped their guns back in their holsters and had their hands out at their sides—well, away from their weapons.

"No, mister, we ain't."

"Glad to hear you got some sense, then."

The one who had not spoken nodded his head slightly, though not in agreement. His curled lip indicated that his nod had simply been a taking of an account which would be paid later.

Both men now started to bring their arms in slowly. Meanwhile, there wasn't a sound in the room. No one even took a drink.

The round barrel of Slocum's Colt .44 moved slightly. "There's that sign says all guns got to be left with the sheriff," he said. "You two fellers drop your guns over here by the sheriff." And he tilted his head toward the prone figure of Deputy Sheriff Hobe Winchy.

He waited while they did so. "Now get out of town."

"But we live here," snapped the one with the sneer.

"Not while I'm in town you don't!"

"What about our guns?"

"The sheriff will take good care of them."

His eyes followed the pair closely all the way through the room and out the batwing doors.

Slocum waited, checking the room carefully. Then he holstered his gun but did not lower his eyes. He stood there listening to the room as the tension began to ease. Presently he bent down and picked up the two guns, plus Hobe Winchy's, and laid them on the bar. Then he turned back to his glass of beer, but with his attention on the room, which was reflected in the big mirror.

He waited a few moments longer while the room returned to normal—more or less—though not for a moment relaxing his vigilance. Meanwhile, Hobe Winchy, lying not far from his feet, had started to stir. Slocum signaled the man behind the bar. "I'm looking for Ben McCormack," he said.

The barman was a reedy-looking individual with a large bandage on his left thumb. "Mister, I dunno."

Slocum leaned forward. "Listen, I tossed my rig in at the East-West House. You ever hear of that place?"

The bartender nodded, his face whitening as his momentary effort at bravado failed. "I'll get the message to him," he said, lowering his voice even more.

He had sunk his hand into the big damp bar rag and had started wiping the top of the bar out of sheer nervousness.

His eyes flicked to the right, then left, and then without looking at Slocum he leaned a little forward. His whisper was hoarse and barely audible. "Mister, that name's not too welcome in this place. I mean, my boss, Mr. Dillingham, don't like him mentioned. I—I don't want any trouble. I just got this job. But I'll give the message to somebody who might know the feller, where he is."

"You better tell him who the message is from," Slocum said.

"I know your name. Heard it before you even come into this place. Slocum—right?"

"John Slocum. Remember the John. Just in case there might be another Slocum in this here country." He stepped back from the bar, lifted his glass, and drained it. "I don't reckon there is, though."

He turned and, with a quick look at the struggling Hobe Winchy, walked out of the saloon.

As he made his way toward the rooming house he realized how deep he already was into something he knew nothing about, nothing at all. And he was thinking how he'd better get a horse before he did anything else. And then he had to find Big Ben McCormack.

4

He had spotted a little buckskin horse in one of the stalls at the livery when the hostler had offered him the bay, and now as he walked toward the rooming house he thought of going down to see what he could work out with the old man—provided the buckskin didn't already have an owner. What he would have preferred of course was a spotted Appaloosa like the one he'd had to shoot. But he decided to wait on it. Besides, Big Ben McCormack would no doubt be a better source than the town livery anyway.

On the way down Main Street he was sure he was being watched. Surely Winchy had buddies, and surely too there would be honest citizens about who wouldn't approve of his beating up a man of the law, even though he was crooked. Anyhow, a lawman's pay was nothing to dance a jig over. Slocum had worn tin. He knew the taste of it. For a lot of people the idea of the law was fine, but carrying it out was something else.

Still, he had run a big risk manhandling Hobe Winchy, even though he was a crook. But he'd made the decision on the spot: that he had to stake out his own position and not back down, not even to the so-called law. Because for sure, somebody was out to kill him—first the two dry-gulchers, then the action at the stage holdup, and finally Winchy's play. What next? And that was always the question.

The East-West was a two-story frame house standing at the edge of town. It had an uncertain look about it, apart from the fact that it could have used a paint job, giving Slocum the feeling now that it had been moved from someplace else. As he approached he realized that it had a slight list to it. Yet it certainly didn't look as though it was about to collapse.

Its location was near what had once been the beginnings of a railroad spur, but with the original closing of the mine the spur had been abandoned. No track had been laid, though a roadbed had come as far as the town. Now it was overgrown, and the East-West stood alone, separated from the town by the abandoned spur.

There was of course a better house at the other end of town, but Slocum preferred being close to the trail, and to the livery, a swift departure from town always being a possibility to keep in mind.

It was the same pasty-faced room clerk behind the desk, looking as though he had trouble even standing up. He was a man in his sixties, Slocum judged, and possibly a lunger. He had that caved-in look, and Slocum remembered that Hardins had been a mining town.

"Forgot to ask when you signed in whether you wanted the room with or without." The wet voice came sighing out of the bent body as the clerk looked over the top of his spectacles at Slocum.

"Depends," Slocum said, taking a good second look at the man behind the desk. He wondered if he was the owner of the East-West. Whatever he was he nevertheless smelled of booze and fried onions.

"You're a man wants to look the merchandise over first, I can see." Something that looked as though it might become a smile entered his face. And he came to life, moving his hands on the desktop, clearing his throat, and then hooking his thin thumbs into his galluses.

"Do you know Ben McCormack?" Slocum asked.

The other man lifted his head now so he could survey Slocum straight on. "Everybody knows Ben McCormack —and nobody does."

Slocum looked into the tight corners of the other man's eyes but said nothing.

"If he's that important to you, mister—Big Ben—then he'll send or"—and his eyes moved up and down his guest —"or he'll come looking for you himself."

Slocum liked the way the old man had changed. Underneath that rheumy, slow-paced tempo and vagueness was a sharp individual who didn't miss a whisker.

Slocum's room was close to the head of the stairs, only a few steps down the dusty, rank-smelling corridor. The house felt as though there weren't many guests.

He locked the door behind him, again taking the room in with a careful glance—nobody had been in it since he'd checked in earlier. Going to the window, he leaned out, checking the alley and looking up to see how far it was to the roof and to the other rooms on each side. Without rope or other help no one could reach his window from outside.

Turning back into the room, he surveyed the brass bed, the washstand with the china bowl and pitcher, the dresser on which stood the coal oil lamp with the dirty chimney. The smell of coal oil was faint in the room, and when he lay down on the bed he was sure the mattress was filled with cornhusks.

He had taken off his gunbelt and slipped the handgun under the pillow, which was damp and smelled of sweat. He didn't mind that, though he preferred the smell of the prairie or high timber. The room had cost two bits, which he'd paid in advance, that being the custom of the country.

Then he got up and set the back of the wooden chair under the doorknob, as an extra precaution. He lay down again, still feeling that something wasn't quite right.

He lay on his back, his thoughts moving carefully through all that had happened from the bushwhacking attempt through the stage holdup and the action in the Only Chance with Hobe Winchy and his buddies.

All the participants had shared one thing in common— they'd known his name. Well, he'd sure been expected in Hardins Crossing. But by whom? Hell, even the bartender in the Only Chance had known who he was. And why was Ben McCormack's name so unpopular? He had thought that the man who had built one of the biggest stage lines in the West would be a household word. Indeed, not long ago he had been. But Slocum had gotten the message in the Only Chance that McCormack was less than welcome. How could that be? Big Ben was—well, a legend. One of the real pioneers, and besides that, a man who had done it himself, a man who wasn't afraid to work or stiff anybody who crossed him. He was a man, after all, who'd once been the bare-knuckle champion of America.

The knock on the door told him that he had dozed off. In a flash he was on his feet, having plucked the Colt from beneath the pillow. Quickly he checked the window as the knock came again.

"Who's there?" he demanded, carefully not standing in front of the door.

"Message for you, Mr. Slocum."

And Slocum felt the agreeable sensation running through him as he recognized the voice. Still, he wasn't biting at any bait. "What is it?"

"Can I come in so I don't have to tell it to the whole town?"

"Are you alone?"

"Just myself and the United States Cavalry."

He stepped close to the door, keeping to one side, and reaching over he removed the chair, then turned the key. At the same time he braced his foot against the bottom of the door and held on to the knob.

"Come in, but the door's stuck, you'll have to push it."

He held his hand on the knob as it was turned, and then resisted the push from outside just for a moment, until he suddenly swept the door open, pulling the surprised girl into the room. He was immediately covering the doorway with his Colt. There was nobody there.

"Jesus Christ!" Honey Mellody was red in the face as her anger burst out at him. "What the hell you tryin' to do? Yank my arm off its socket?"

"Just making sure you were alone, Honey."

"Right now I wish I was!"

Slocum shut the door and locked it and turned toward her. "I thought it might be you, but then, you never know for sure."

She was wildly out of breath, and Slocum was following each intake and outgoing of her magnificent bosom.

"What can I do for you?" he said, stepping further into the center of the room. "What's the message?"

"A friend asked me to deliver it from Mr. McCormack."

"A friend? Why not McCormack?"

"Because he's not in town. And don't ask me any more questions."

"So what's the message?"

She bent down and lifted her skirt, and making no pretense at turning away from him she drew up her petticoat and unpinned a folded piece of paper. "This tells how to get where he is. He isn't in town."

"You already said that." Slocum took the paper and opened it. It was a simple map leading him north from Hardins to the fork of a river.

"What is it? A cattle outfit?"

"I don't know anything," she said. "Except he wanted me to take you there."

"Don't you know where it is?"

She didn't answer, but he saw her lower lip tremble.

But he didn't let his tone of voice soften when he said, "Sit down." And then he added, "Here. On the chair."

He sat on the edge of the bed facing her, carefully taking in every move she made, every expression on her face. Even so, he couldn't keep from thinking how good-looking she was. "You McCormack's girl?"

She started to speak, and then suddenly her tears came. She lowered her head, now holding a handkerchief to her eyes. Gone totally was the assured young woman of the stagecoach who had ordered the young male passenger to leave his derringer on the floor.

But Slocum learned that Honey Mellody had fiber in her backbone, if not rawhide. There was a new tone in her voice when she said, "Why you ask that? You interested?" And she cocked her head at him, with a new look in her eyes.

Slocum could have picked up on it, but he decided

McCormack was the important thing right now, not to mention taking care of his own hide. For he was sure Hobe Winchy wasn't going to take his beating lying down, and there was Print and his stagecoach buddies as well. Slocum knew from long experience how he would have to watch his back. Plus, there was the sheriff. How sick was he? And would he hit the path when he got wind of how his deputy had been whipsawed?

"I want to know where McCormack is, and why you're here, here in my room."

She pointed to the paper that was lying beside him on the bed. "That's where he is. I just showed you. And I'm here in your room to tell you that. And that's all I know, mister!" He watched the anger kindling in her blue eyes now, and thought again how good-looking she was.

"Just slow it a minute. I want to hear you talk. Tell me about McCormack. What is he to you, and you to him? Are you working for him? Is he still running stages? Is that his ranch out there? Why doesn't anybody in the Only Chance want to talk about him?" And as he spoke, a part of him was listening to the corridor outside. Was she part of a trap?

"Why don't you wait till we get out there and ask him yourself?" she was saying.

And now Slocum leaned hard into his words. "Because I'm asking you. And I am asking you right here and right now!"

But she didn't back down. By gosh, he was thinking, this gal has sand in her craw. He admired that. Not many you met like this.

"Golly!" she said suddenly, and her eyes were round and big with astonishment. "You're a one, ain't you! I always thought men wanted to do it, not sit around and talk a streak!"

Slocum had a rough time keeping a straight face, but he managed. "How come everybody in the whole damn country seemed to know I was heading for Hardins? Who was the owlhoot I braced on the stage? Start with him. Print, he said his name was."

"I don't know who he was. I'm telling you the truth."

"But he knew you."

"I think so." She nodded, and her brow knitted as though she was trying to think of something. "I know I've seen him before. Though his face was covered. And that Texas voice."

"Hell, that was fake!"

She shrugged. "So he knew you too!"

"I know McCormack's in some big action, and it looks to me like somebody was trying to hurt him by swiping his gal."

"Well, thanks to you, you big, strong he-man, he didn't get away with it!" And she stuck her tongue out at him, making a wild face.

"How long have you known Ben McCormack?"

"Long enough to like him."

"He told you to bring me out to wherever he's at."

"Goddamn it! Didn't I just tell you that!"

"Just wanted to be sure you remembered your own story," Slocum said easily. "And I'm still trying to get the whole of it out of you."

"The whole of what! I've told you the whole thing! Big Ben wanted me to bring you to where he's at, and that's what I'm here for. I think."

"Right. But now—when did he tell you that?"

She looked down at her hands, which she was holding together on her knees.

"Did you know who I was on the stage?"

"No! Look, I swear it. I had no notion who you were.

Never even heard the name Slocum before. I was just riding the stage back from Justin, and those mugs tried to pull me off it. So I got you to thank. So has McCormack, I guess."

"What were you doing out at Justin?"

"That's my private business."

"You were out there on something for McCormack," he insisted.

"Why don't you ask him all about it, will you?"

Slocum got up suddenly and walked to the window and looked out.

When he turned back into the room she said, "I got the message from Ben when I was at the depot here in Hardins. Somehow he knew you were on the stage. Or maybe he didn't. Anyway, I think he wanted to make sure you were really the one he was expecting. Something like that. He's got a lot of people making trouble for him."

"I think I figured that much out," Slocum said wryly. "And he's holed up."

She nodded. "I figure he was thinkin' if you came out with me you'd maybe fool them. I mean, like you were taking me someplace." And to his astonishment she flushed with embarrassment.

"And if I went alone the chances were they'd pick me off?"

"I don't know."

"Or if you went out there alone they'd get you. That doesn't make sense, for they'd get us both, which is what they want. Except they want you alive."

"I don't know."

"So they can put the squeeze on McCormack."

"Ben got hurt bad. He's laid up. Got shot at and his horse threw him and kicked him."

"Is he all right, or is he out of it?"

"He's coming around. But meanwhile he's not here to handle things."

"Things?"

"Ben practically runs, or used to run, Hardins—with the council too, I mean. But this man Dillingham's been trying to move in. Dillingham's got a lot of money, and he owns the Only Chance and some other properties in town and around."

"Who is Dillingham?"

"I don't know, Slocum, believe me. I wish you'd talk to Big Ben. Something about the stage line. I dunno what. But lay off me, will you?"

He thought she was going to cry again as she dabbed at her eyes, but she handled herself. "Hell," she said.

"Come here," he said. He was standing just away from the window. "See that man down there?"

"Yeah. What about him?"

"You know him?"

"Never saw him before. He watching or something? Slocum, let's get out of here."

"That's what I'm aiming to do." He looked at the map again. "How far is it?"

"I don't know how long it would take. I've never been there. See that big brick house when we came in?"

"I couldn't miss it."

"That's Ben's place when he's in town."

"Does he ever come in anymore?"

"I don't know. See, this man Dillingham, like I said, he wants to take over the town, and he's got gunmen. But so has Ben. But Ben doesn't want to shoot it out, I guess, leastways from what I've heard from him. Though he sure isn't backing down. But he's trying to get something going. He'll tell you. I dunno what it is."

"Out there is it?"

"Slocum, I dunno. All I know is he's told me to bring you out to his place up on the North Fork. I mean, I was to give you the map and we'd both go. I dunno how to get there."

"Who gave you the map?"

"One of his men, I guess it was. I dunno."

"Then why doesn't he take us out there?"

"I dunno! Jesus, I dunno!"

He had crossed to the door and was listening.

She watched him, biting her lower lip. "Slocum, if that man's waiting down there, watching this place, let's get the hell out of here."

Slocum had returned to the window.

"What's he doing down there?"

"Watching this place and picking his nose."

"Can we go?"

"Two of those horses at that hitch rail outside the saloon look pretty good from here."

"Slocum, for Christ's sake, this is no time to be looking at horses!"

"You want to walk to the North Fork?"

And now he crossed the room again and stood next to the door, listening. When she started to speak, he held up his hand to silence her.

When he turned back to her he said, "Why aren't you taking your clothes off?"

She stared at him with her mouth open. "You crazy? With that feller down in the street, and like you're thinkin' somebody's at the door maybe?"

He said nothing in answer to her outburst but just stood there watching her.

"What the hell's the matter with you?" she demanded furiously.

"Isn't that what you came up here for?"

"You're crazy!"

He said nothing, and she could see he was listening toward the corridor. Then he faced her. "Just checking you," he said. "A man can't be too careful."

"And—a woman!"

He grinned suddenly. "You look to be pretty good at taking care of yourself," he said. "In fact, you look pretty good."

"Gee, thanks, Mr. Slocum, sir."

But he saw that he had touched her.

"This'll be the third time since yesterday someone's tried to kill me."

"You lead a thrilling life," she said. "I'm glad I don't share it."

His grin returned, and he gave a silent laugh. "Well, if you want to get out of here without getting caught by whoever was running that fake stage holdup you're going to be sharing it with me." He looked at her thoughtfully. "And lady, you could do a lot worse."

"Let's get out of here, Slocum."

"We'll wait a spell."

"You're crazy!"

"I don't want to disappoint the boys."

"Who you talkin' about?"

"The ones on the way up here to find you and me all cozy together in bed."

"Goddamn it, I told you I didn't have anything to do with that kind of a setup."

"I believe you. But that's what they're counting on."

"Jesus . . ." said Honey Mellody.

"Get into bed," he said, stepping away from the window, where he had seen the three men come out of the Eagle

Saloon and walk over to the man who had been watching the East-West.

"Boy, you have got the craziest ideas, mister!"

"Just lie on top, but start making noises like you were having a good time—when I tell you. They'll be a couple of minutes getting up here."

"The men you're expecting. Our guests."

He had gone back to the window. "That's right. And if I can go by my hunch I'll wager those horses are theirs. They must have stolen them."

He was at the door again. "Start moaning. Make it sound real good."

"You got to do it too."

He had picked up the chair and now pulled it apart, so that one of the legs split, making a point like a spear.

The girl was already making the sounds of sex on the bed, rolling around a bit to help her act, the bed creaking wildly. Slocum joined in with a couple of yelps of joy. He watched her for a short moment, it was a damn good act she was putting on. Then he stood back against the wall right beside the door.

All at once the door burst open and Slocum smashed the first man to enter right on the back of his neck with the chair leg. The rabbit punch knocked him flat onto the floor. The second man he kicked in the shins and drove the wicked point of the broken chair leg into his side. The man let out a scream of pain.

The third man had swung his gun at Slocum's head, grazing him and knocking him back. But Slocum had staged the field of combat, and he had brought the surprise. He was counting too on the fact that they wouldn't want to harm the girl and so wouldn't fire into the bed.

The first man was on the floor out cold. The second was on his knees, grabbing his side where the point of the broken chair leg had stabbed him. The third man was just lifting his gun into line to shoot Slocum.

Slocum ducked and threw the chair leg right at the other man's crotch. It was no mortal blow, or even very harmful, but it brought distraction. It gave Slocum the split moment he needed to shift his stance and throw a piledriver right into his assailant's neck. The man's gun went off; the bullet went through the floor and was received with a scream of pain from the room below. Slocum brought over a left and then a right into his attacker's belly, and then smashed him right behind his ear. It took only a minute to see that two of his attackers were Hobe Winchy's buddies from the Only Chance. The third man was a stranger.

"It's all clear," Honey said from the doorway, where she had taken a position as a lookout.

Together they ran down the corridor and down the stairs.

"You watch my stuff," Slocum snapped at the room clerk. "I'll be back with some questions on why you let those bastards in!"

"Hold it right there!"

It was the man who had been watching from the street. He was standing in the doorway with his six-gun in his hand. "Lucky I began to suspicion something," he said, and he was obviously enjoying his triumph.

But now the shot that rang out came from the stairway behind Slocum and Honey Mellody, and they watched the man in the doorway crumble, his own gun going off and shooting him in the foot.

"Is that the sonofabitch shot me through the ceiling, goddamn it!" It was T. Wellington Throneberry standing there on the stairway with a pistol in his hand. There was blood on his face. "Sonofabitch creased me. Damn him! Damn him! Upstart! Do you reckon he was one of that ridiculous gang that tried to hold us up, Mr. Washington, sir?"

His thick white eyebrows arched in indignation as he moved down the stairway. He was wearing a remarkable plaid coat, the plaid interrupted in a number of places by tears in the cloth, plus a number of stains, visible now as he came into the brighter light of the foyer.

Slocum turned to the room clerk. "That feller's still alive, so you better get the doc, and get his buddies to handle it when they come to."

And he was out the door, with the girl at his heels, but not running, going carefully. It was dusk, and the shots had attracted nobody's attention. But Slocum knew he couldn't count on the men upstairs staying out for any length of time.

"Why are we going so slow?" the girl asked impatiently.

"Don't want to attract a lot of attention. So just walk easy. You take that black mare and I'll take him." He was standing beside the spotted pony he'd seen from the window of his room. There were three other horses at the hitch rail, and quickly he pulled out his bowie knife and cut halfway through their cinches. The boys were due for a nice spill when they tried to mount up.

Then he was up on the spotted horse and they were going at a fast walk toward the end of town. Even before the street ended they were breaking into a canter. And in another moment Slocum had lifted his horse to a full gallop. The girl followed suit. He was glad to see that she could handle a horse.

5

They rode that night until the sky began to lighten. By then Slocum was sure they weren't being followed. The spotted horse proved to be as good as he had hoped— fast, durable, and obviously well broken for working cattle.

Now they had camped in a high place where he could see anyone approaching across a long strip of prairie, while their back was covered by the high timber.

"Can we build a fire?" the girl asked.

"You hungry?"

"I could take some coffee."

"Good enough," he said. "You build the fire and I'll picket our horses. Feed's good, and they need the rest, too."

He picketed the black and the spotted horse, first stripping them and then giving each a rubdown with

53

some twigs that were handy in the nearby timber. They were just by the timberline, and above that rimrocks began to come into view as the morning reached into the sky.

"Keep the fire down," he said, coming up to her when he was done. "Use some green stuff now."

"You think we're being followed?"

"It's sensible to figure you're being followed, even if you're not," he said.

From where they sat, with their backs protected and with the long sweep of land before them, they would be able to see anyone approaching. It was a good place. He was glad for the rest, and he saw that the girl was tired.

"We'll get some sleep," he said.

"I could use it." She was looking at him as he drank the last of his coffee.

"Should be there in a few hours," Slocum said. "Looks from the map like it's beyond that butte yonder."

He had lain down on his back and taken off his hat. The coughing bark of a coyote broke the silence then, and he closed his eyes.

He felt her coming, her step seeming like a vibration on the soft ground. And then she was kneeling beside him, and the touch of her lips on his was sweet.

"I can't help it, Slocum." Her breath was warm on his eyes. "I want to lie down with you."

He shifted onto his side and slid his arm around her. She was almost trembling.

"My God, I'm so hot for you," she whispered.

Slocum said nothing, for there was nothing to say. He reached down and began unbuttoning her blouse. In a moment that seemed endless her cool, firm breast was in his big hand, the nipple hard, the breast itself thrusting out from her body. He bent his head, and she slipped her hand behind him to draw him down onto her two breasts.

"Suck them. Oh God, bite them, suck, bite . . ."

He obliged, his organ almost splitting his trousers as her hand busily unbuttoned him and struggled to get his huge erection out into play. And then she was down on it, taking it deep into her mouth, down her throat, licking and sucking and playing with his balls, as with any free hand that was about they tore off their clothes.

He had his hand in her bush and had pulled down her pants. She had a lot of hair, and her slit was soaking wet, absolutely ready for mounting.

There was no waiting now as he flipped her onto her back and her legs sprang wide, her knees up as he brought his cock right into her vagina. Grabbing his buttocks she pulled him in, though he was already thrusting. Deep, high, he pushed as far as he could go, hitting bottom, and rubbing the head of his organ there while she squirmed and squealed with total abandon, digging her nails into his buttocks, bucking her loins with his in a quickening rhythm which was bringing them both to a frenzy.

"Don't hold back!" she begged. "Come! Come with me! I'm ready, I'm ready. Please, Slocum . . . Slo . . . cum . . . come . . ."

Their loins were now thrashing to a crescendo of extinction, as he rode her hard, then easy, then slowly and gently, and then quicker until he flooded her, and she him. Their come was all over their bellies as they collapsed into stupefied, ecstatic exhaustion.

They slept.

The man had just survived being thrown and then tromped by a tough, mean bronc, a battering that would have killed just about anybody else. But the man lying on the pile of buffalo robes had once been the bare-knuckle champion of America, and he had suffered worse and had lived through it.

Big Ben McCormack attracted difficulties, trouble, excitement, drama. He was one of those rare ones who live life all the way. Indeed, his presence in life verified the adage that it is not the weak who need help, for everybody helps the weak, but it is the strong, who everyone thinks can handle anything that comes. And indeed, they do. But at a cost. The latest cost to Big Ben McCormack had been his health.

All the same, strong or weak, it didn't matter to Big Ben, for he made his own rules and fought his own fights. He never asked for quarter, and rarely gave any. And perhaps on those rare occasions he only gave enough to prove he was human after all.

He was surely not asking for quarter now as he lay impatiently on those heavy buffalo robes while his great body healed. Now from the pocket of his coat, which was lying beside him, he took out his big gold watch with its five-pound chain of solid gold and studied the time.

"You sure she got my message," he said, more in assertion of his orders than in questioning.

The woman he had spoken to had been bent over her sewing. She looked up and her eyes met his. "I gave it to Tony, and he said he'd delivered it. He just got back about an hour ago. You were asleep so I didn't tell you."

Big Ben let out an enormous sigh, trying to handle his frustration. He lay immobile now, his eyes closed. He was in his middle fifties but still possessed much of the vigor of his youth.

The woman had stopped sewing and now sat quietly watching this man who had taken her for his wife. She was in her early forties, but she, contrary to her husband, looked older than her years. For one thing her body was somewhat bent as a result of a difficult stillbirth, which also caused her to limp; and part of one side of her face—mostly hidden by the way she did her hair—carried a scarlet birthmark. Yet her eyes were bright, though on close inspection one would have realized the sadness in them. As she watched her husband now, and while a snore rolled out of him as he slept, her eyes and the whole expression on her face had changed. The only word that could have described what was so evident was the word love. Candida McCormack loved her husband, not because of her own solitude, or her misfortune, but simply because it was her nature. She loved him, his great, hearty laugh, his pitch-black moods, his drinking, his brawling, his infidelities. She loved him. She loved him, too, in spite of Honey Mellody. She longed for him to take her to bed. It had been a long time since he had embraced her.

Realizing suddenly that he was no longer asleep, she bent quickly to her sewing, feeling the flush of her desire pulsing up around her ears, and in her loins. She could feel his eyes on her.

Big Ben looked again at his watch.

"Can I get you anything?" Candida asked.

"No. No—I'm all right." He sniffed, scratched himself, digging deep. He swore silently, victimized by his impatience, his turning thoughts. And that was it; to be . . . all right. Him! Who could fight like a wildcat, drink a bottle of whiskey without turning a hair, and ride! But now! Stove up, just like some old boozed-up bronc stomper.

Reaching again to his coat he took out a cigar and struck a lucifer and lighted it. Ah, that was better! He

watched the balloon of smoke rising to the ceiling of the
room, thinking now of the home he'd had on Nob Hill in
San Francisco. Ah, that was a mansion all right. He had
built it with hallways a team of horses could be driven
through. He'd ordered it, by God! His coach teams and
his stable of racehorses had been the envy of all. And
those other mansions in Denver, Kansas City, Chicago!
Ah, those days! Those days when his vast transportation
system had all but spanned the continent. He had ribboned the West, competing neck and neck with the likes
of Wells Fargo and Butterfield. Guts, it had taken! And
brains. And guile, too! The smaller business problems
he'd handled with his big fists, while for the bigger af-
fairs he had always become a different Ben McCormack
—a suave gentleman of charm and sleight of hand. Yet
he had always preferred the former role, the role that had
developed from his early life as a stableboy and mine
mucker in the toughest towns of the West. It had led him
to the championship of America. Top man with his fists!
Ah, that was living. That had been living. And it would
be again.

In the morning they did it again. She had told him she liked
it a certain way especially; and Slocum, being an obliging
gentleman, had gone along with that and more.

   Now, as they rode down the steep, winding trail toward
the North Fork of the Horse Gap River, he was feeling that
wonderful sense of himself in his whole body.

   The day was spectacular. The tops of the high mountains standing in the great blue sky, the smell of sage and
their horses, the warm touch of a stirring breeze now and
again on his face and hands—all added up to why he was
here at this particular time, in this particular place. Looking for a man named Big Ben McCormack, who must be

having trouble with his stage line, else why would he have wanted Slocum.

As he rode now he found the pieces coming together —the attempted drygulching where he'd lost his spotted horse and damn near himself to boot, the man named Print and his stopping the stage presumably to take the girl as a hostage, and the toughs and deputy at the Only Chance Saloon, and finally the action at the East-West House, which had netted him a damn fine cow pony. And by no means to forget that extra bonus, Miss Honey Mellody.

He watched her now, liking the way she handled her horse, admiring her looks, the way the wisps of blond hair flew into her eyes and the way she brushed those wisps aside. She had good hands, too. Slocum liked a woman to have good hands, plus a few other "good" things, of course.

"I want to do it again," she said suddenly drawing rein.

Slocum was doubly surprised by her remark since he'd been thinking precisely the same thing.

"So would I," he said. "But it's daylight, and we have to get where we're going."

They both sat their horses now, in the shade of a stand of aspen. Slocum still kept a wary eye on their back trail and all the surrounding country.

"I want to especially," Honey said, shifting her weight in her saddle.

"What do you mean—'especially'?"

"I mean we won't be able to do it when we get to Ben's place."

"Then you are McCormack's girl?"

She made a face, then frowned. "I guess so, leastways when I'm with him. I'd better warn you, Slocum, Mr.

McCormack doesn't like anyone fooling around with whatever he considers his personal property."

"So you're his personal property, are you?"

"Ben figures I am."

"And you?"

She looked at him directly now. "Mr. Slocum, I am only a poor working girl—beautiful, intelligent, passionate—but a poor working girl. And I know what side my bread's buttered on."

"Got'cha." Slocum couldn't help grinning at her.

And now he saw something more than just her courage and aggressiveness, something in the way she was holding her lower lip, tucked in without actually biting it, plus a certain expression in her blue eyes.

He squinted at the sky. "No sense in running weight off the horses," he said. "Now is there?"

And her laugh was soft like a touch as they both kneed their ponies toward the stand of aspen and box elders.

"So you let him get away with it!" Quince Dillingham leaned back in his big leather chair and leveled his hard little eyes at the man standing in front of his desk.

"I didn't let him get away with nothing," Print LeJeune insisted. "It was like I told you. He had that gun right up my nose like. He coulda blown my head off, I mean right now!"

"He outplayed you, Print. He slickered you neat as a wild deuce." Suddenly Dillingham leaned forward, laying his forearms on top of the papers on his desk. "A little job like taking that woman Mellody and you mess it up. Hell, man, you had Jason and Flanagan backing you!"

"Boss, how did I know he was gonna be on that stage! I thought Pickens and Tommy took care of him."

The man at the desk, dressed all in black, leaned back

in his chair now. "They buggered it even worse than you. I see I'll have to get somebody competent to handle things."

"Boss, I can take him."

"I don't like jokes, Print."

"Mr. Dillingham, I will kill that sonofabitch anytime you say so."

The man at the desk had been looking down at his fingernails, and now he lifted his narrow face to peer at the man standing before him. "I know, Print. I know you will. But when I tell you. Now get out of here, I've got some thinking to do. Some thinking that will have to rectify the mess you've made of things."

The man standing in front of the big desk let his breath out now, now that he felt the dangerous moment had passed.

"Did Mellody recognize you? Or anyone else for that matter?"

"I dunno. I don't think so. I wore a bandanna and I disguised my voice."

A smile of frozen incredulity swept into the other man's face. "Jesus," he murmured softly, but not apparently to anyone in particular.

When the door closed behind Print LeJeune, Quince Dillingham ran the palms of his hands over his smooth black hair. He was a large man yet gangly, and strangely graceful in movement. Now when he shifted his weight in his chair his face twisted in a grimace as he banged his knee on the leg of the table that stood at a right angle to the desk and was covered with several opened maps.

Quincy Dillingham, the scion of a wealthy eastern family, was a man of forty years. His long frame appeared to carry more bone than flesh, yet he was vigorous, with a passion for perfection that was equaled only by his insatiable physical appetites. He loved good food, though he didn't have an inch of unnecessary fat on him, and he loved wine and spirits, good cigars, racehorses, pit dogs, target shooting, and last, and in reality first—women. His tastes, where the pleasures of the flesh were concerned, were various. He marveled at variety, not to mention sexual skill. At the same time there was something else he treasured, and which had eluded him throughout his lifetime search for power and bliss. This was something he could not describe; indeed, he claimed that it was indescribable. He sought innocence in a woman. Strange, he often mused, strange this particular taste, for the more he sought after it, the further it seemed to recede. Yet now, to his astonishment, one more opportunity to attain his goal had appeared.

He had first seen her in the street only this spring. To his delight he learned that the one doctor in Hardins Crossing happened to be her father. And even better, he had discovered that Dr. Barney owned land—including a fair-sized log house and a barn only a few miles from town. This property, however, lay in the direct path of a struggle over water rights at the South Fork of the Horse Gap river. The ranchers involved were pressuring the doctor, though not too strongly in view of the fact that he was the only medical man for miles around; but the water they needed ran mostly on Doc Barney's acres. Doc was no problem, but the warring factions around him were. In short, this imbroglio was just what Quince Dillingham needed to give him an opening toward Jilly Barney. And shortly, after helping the doctor with his legal difficulties, he had worked his way into Jilly's good graces, and the couple were betrothed. To Dillingham's delight and astonishment the girl proved even more innocent than he had hoped for.

It was a major coup—a real beauty, an innocent beauty. Beauty and the beast! His droll description made him chuckle.

Quincy, just now wrapped in a daydream about the young girl who had—he had to admit, rather matter-of-factly—agreed to become his wife, suddenly found himself wondering if she had some ulterior motive. But he swept such an idiotic thought from his mind as he was interrupted by a knock at the door of his office.

"Who is it?"

And he remembered he had made an appointment with Stella. He rose swiftly to his feet, his immediate, lurid vision of Jilly Barney dissolving into the atmosphere as he strode to the door and opened it. "Do come in, my dear."

The redheaded girl who walked in smiled discreetly, against the possibility of someone else being present in the office; and then seeing that there wasn't, as Dillingham closed the door behind her, her face broke into a grin.

"Have a seat, my dear," Dillingham said, and turning back he locked the door, then walked quickly to his desk.

"Business before pleasure!"

"Ekh!" But she smiled as she sat down in the chair he indicated and crossed her legs. She was wearing a simple calico dress, and her full bosom stretched the simple design out of shape. She had a wide face with high cheekbones, large brown eyes, and full red lips. Quince Dillingham found her a highly satisfactory partner for his sexual needs.

"You realize we cannot spend much time together, my dear. I'm scheduled for dinner with my fiancée."

Stella pouted, flipping her handkerchief at him, for she

knew he was teasing. "Let her wait, honeybun."

"Now let's get down to business," he said quickly, his erection straining at his trousers while he moved some of the papers on his desk. "Give me your news."

"The man—Slocum. Well, like you probably already know, he was in the Only Chance and beat up on Hobe Winchy and a couple of his buddies."

"I know that."

"Then he really fixed the boys at the East-West. You sent them, did you?"

"My dear, no unnecessary questions, please. And anyway, you're not telling me anything I don't know already. Give me something new."

"Slocum and the girl took off on stolen horses."

"Now that's interesting." Dillingham's eyebrows lifted. "Whose?"

"The boys who tried to give him a going-over in his hotel room."

A thin smile touched Dillingham's thin lips. "Tit for tat, eh?" His eyes fell onto the girl's bosom as she took a deep breath and settled herself more comfortably in her chair. "Anything else?"

"Only that the town is buzzing. I mean, Hardins is no cream-cake town, but this feller Slocum has stood 'em on their ear. I mean, Tom O'Whales was saying in the Only Chance the man's all buffalo bone and whang leather."

Quince Dillingham was grinning. "Quite, my dear. But there is a sure cure for that kind of thing."

"Yeah?" Her eyes twinkled and she kicked up her leg just a little as it lay crossed over her knee. "What? Girls?"

Quince was not grinning. He was looking hard at her.

"Lead," he said. He let a pause enter the room and then he added slowly, "One has to always be careful about lead, my dear. Lead poisoning is a sure killer."

"I was only joking, honeybun," she pouted. "Don't take everything I say so seriously. I was only funning."

"I was not."

He stood up and walked around the desk and stood facing her. She remained seated, her legs still crossed, with her eyes on the bulge in his trousers.

"Let's take a lot of time," she said as she reached out and cupped her hand over his erection. Then she reached up and began unbuttoning his fly.

"The door is locked," he said.

"What a pity," the girl said, as she came down onto the floor on her knees and reached into his trousers.

"Is that it?" the girl asked.

Slocum nodded, his eyes sweeping the long draw to the log cabin, the round horse corral, and the barn. "That's how your map says it. Looks to be a line camp."

Honey Mellody shifted her weight. "I'll sure be glad to get out of this saddle."

Slocum didn't answer.

"I said—"

He held up his hand to silence her. He had pulled the spotted horse back into the box elders and now signaled her to do the same with the black. She could hear nothing, nor was there any sign of movement down at the cabin.

After a moment she whispered, "What is it?"

"Somebody's cut our trail. I dunno whether it's one of McCormack's riders or maybe some more of our friends who appear so interested in what I'm doing."

"Golly, I—"

"Don't move!" His whisper was like steel, and she saw

him nod toward something across the long, wide draw. "Over there—just by that big bullberry bush."

"I don't see anything." She was straining out of her saddle.

"He's gone now."

"What . . . who?"

"Injun. Likely Arapaho, but maybe Crow. He wasn't painted up, so he might just have been having a look-see."

"Slocum, I'm scared. I'm a town person. What the hell am I doing way the hell out here with wild Indians and gunmen all over the place!"

He could see the strain in her white face, and the way she was gripping the reins of her pony.

"I guess you're out here on account of Mr. Ben McCormack."

"I guess so." And then she said, "Want you to know I enjoyed your company, Slocum."

"Anytime, young lady." And he grinned at her as he kneed the spotted horse and they started down the draw.

He had his hand on his six-gun all the way down, but nothing happened. "I guess he was just looking," he said, as they quartered down to the ranch in the late-afternoon sunlight.

"Like you say, Slocum, I'm Ben's woman, but . . ."

"I got'cha."

Neither of them said anything more as they worked their way down toward the big bearded man standing in the doorway of the log cabin with the Winchester in his hands.

"You can grain 'em in the barn, an' picket 'em by the creek." Big Ben growled his greeting.

Slocum told him about the Indian at the top of the draw.

"That was Standing Horse. He works for me. Not so

noticed as a regular cowhand," he said. "You got sharp eyes, Slocum."

Slocum nodded and took the black pony's reins as Honey Mellody slid down from the saddle.

As Slocum rode off to the barn, leading the black, Honey turned to McCormack. "Why ain't you lying down?"

"Like to give up on your gettin' here 'fore sundown," the big bearded man said, ignoring her question. He was drinking her in with his eyes. "Been a while, Honey."

"How is Candy?"

He nodded. "She's all right. Took good care of me, though not the way you can."

"I'm here now."

He bent toward her quickly and gave her a peck on the cheek. His hand touched her shoulder lightly. She knew he didn't want to be seen by Candy yet couldn't restrain himself. Ben, she knew, could never restrain himself. It was one of the things she liked so much about him.

When they entered the cabin, she saw that Candy wasn't there. She nodded toward the bedroom.

"Candy," Ben called. "We got our company here at last."

"I saw." The soft voice preceded her through the doorway. How are you, Honey?"

"Good. Good to see you, Candy."

"Honey can help get supper," McCormack said.

"Ben, you've got to lie down. You shouldn't be up at all, let alone walking about." Candida had approached him, limping.

"I ain't tired," Ben said, and he started toward the corral. "Want to see this feller that I've been hearing so much about."

The women waited a moment, seemingly undecided how to be, but then Candy turned back toward the kitchen and Honey followed her.

Through the open barn door Slocum saw McCormack approaching slowly. He had found some cloth and was getting ready to give the horses a rubdown. They were already stripped, and when McCormack's big shape darkened the doorway he was bent down checking the spotted horse's shoes.

"Got yerself a good piece of horseflesh there, I'd say." Big Ben's deep voice seemed to fill the barn. "That little black one, though, she's just about makin' it."

"Had my doubts about her," Slocum said, letting go of the foot he'd been holding. "But she'll be all right."

"Had some trouble in town, did you?"

Slocum touched on the high points of what had happened, starting with the two bushwhackers, through the stage holdup and the fights in the saloon and in his hotel room.

"You lead an exciting life, Slocum."

"Hardins an exciting town. I figure somebody knew I was coming."

"Know anything about who was behind it? Different people, or the same party?" Big Ben had moved into the barn as Slocum began wiping down the spotted horse.

"Figure it's likely the same one behind it. And looks to be connected with whatever it is you wanted to see me about."

"That's the way I size it." McCormack had moved to a crate that was standing near some harness hanging from the wall nearest Slocum. With a grunt he sat down, the crate creaking under his weight. "The women are cookin' up some grub," he said. "And I'll be putting up something to whet our whistle."

"Good enough," Slocum said. He stood there looking squarely at McCormack, deciding that he liked the man. "I'll just do the mare."

"Take your time." Big Ben spat in the direction of a scurrying pack rat. "We got plenty to do, so no point hurrying it."

They fell silent now, the two of them, each feeling the other, the way men do at such times. And when Slocum was through with the black mare he tossed the rags back into the corner where he'd found them.

A sickle moon was out as the last light was leaving the sky on their way up from the barn to the house. They moved slowly, Ben cussing now and again at himself. The coming evening was cool on their hands and faces, and the smell of everything in the land filled them.

Looking toward the cabin, Slocum saw one of the women at a window lighting a coal oil lamp. Then he realized it was McCormack's wife, and he was all at once struck by a remarkable beauty.

6

"That was the stage line I started for Brigham Young, from Atchinson to Salt Lake. I mean, he wanted it, but I built it."

The big man was expansive, back in his old form, Slocum realized, as under the warmth of the two women, plus the good whiskey and cigars, the evening progressed.

"I figured on a coach line that'd crowd the Pony Express for speed. So I got me built the finest coaches, the fastest teams, the best men, and on top of that, well-stocked relay stations, and close together—like twelve miles apart in the wilderness, by God. Cost me a fortune. But by golly in those days I had it. And I spent it."

"I always heard you delivered the best," Slocum said.

Big Ben McCormack beamed as he reached for his glass of whiskey. "Picked the horses and mules each one myself. The Concords cost me fifteen hundred dollars each! Hell, the passengers got served the best food ever at any rest stop. The trick was, I rode the lines myself, and without anybody beknownst I was doin' it. So nobody ever tried shortchanging on service or the quality neither." He grunted, ran his hand over his black beard, and hunched his shoulders, which were as big as cannonballs. "People used to claim I was spending too damn much on matched teams when I could've got common horseflesh for a lot less; but hell, Slocum, you've seen them Injun ponies. Runty, and gaunted and half-starved on bunch grass. Good horseflesh outran them crowbaits over and over again. Had to, by God!"

They had finished dinner and were now sitting in the front room of the cabin while the women cleared up and washed. McCormack was on his second cigar, Slocum still with his first.

Suddenly there was a lull in the one-sided conversation. It was silent in the room. Slocum could hear the clink of cutlery and pots in the kitchen. The man seated before him had stopped as suddenly as a charging buffalo hit with a Sharps.

"Better lie down a spell," he said. And he stood up, carefully, and moved toward the buffalo robes in the corner of the room. "Come over here. Bring your chair." Big Ben was wheezing some.

Then Candida was at the door. "Ben, I told you!" But her words were more sad than sharp. "I told you not to get up. But you never listen! Now lie down. What can I get you?"

"A whiskey."

"No—some hot milk is more in order."

Slocum almost laughed aloud at the grimace McCormack made.

"None of that goddamn milk!" He cleared his throat

loudly. "Now, somebody wants to give me a nice tit to suck on, that might be more like it!"

"Ben McCormack, you stop that talk! Right now!"

Candida was red in the face, and as she led him toward the buffalo robes, her limp seemed more aggravated.

"Only funnin', my dear. Only funnin'." And a rich chuckle broke from him.

But Slocum could see that she was pleased—pleased, it seemed, by any kind of attention from her man.

When the woman had left them and they were alone again, Slocum moved his chair over to where Big Ben was lying on his back.

"So what can I do for you?" he said. "Or do you want to wait till the morning?"

"Hell no, I don't want to wait till morning! We got too damn much to talk about! I was just waitin' to be shut of them women so's we could talk freely. Hell, I didn't write you to come all the hell the way out here at the end of nowheres to wait till morning, for Christ sake!"

"I'm listening," Slocum said, accepting the bottle that his host now passed, and which had been hidden in the buffalo robes.

"Honey was—all right, was she? During the holdup?"

Slocum thought he heard concern in the big man's voice, but wasn't sure. McCormack was not a man given to sentiment, but Slocum had caught the feeling the moment he'd entered the cabin that here was a man who surely might have more than one woman in his life at any particular moment, but he would always treat them right.

"She was good. Handled herself really good," Slocum said. "Fact, she straightened a young dude who thought of pulling a derringer."

A chuckle rose in McCormack's throat as Slocum described the scene.

"And this other feller—Throneberry, you mentioned. I know him. He's a waspy old bugger."

"But he's new around Hardins."

"If he's the same feller. I knew him down around Santa Fe. Dealt three-card monte at the Daffodil. But I never knew him close." He sniffed. "Wonder what he's doin' here."

Then he seemed to shake himself, once again giving Slocum the impression of a feisty old buffalo.

"Lemme get to the nubbin'. You know I got one stage route left—Butte down to Horse Gap through Hardins and on down to Cheyenne. South and east."

Slocum nodded.

"The railroad's killed us, Slocum. Just when I had my competitors by the balls—mostly Wells Fargo, and I was really raking in the pot. Hell, the railroads been ribboning the whole damn country. Now there's talk of a line east from Cheyenne to St. Jo; on this end up from Cheyenne to Hardins Crossing. That'd make Hardins a shipping point for Texas cattle."

"The stagecoach is finished, then."

"Not yet. No, sir! Not yet!"

"Then you're going to fight them."

Big Ben took a long pull on his drink. "You bet your ass. So long as there's life in me I'll fight. Look, this country's doing fine with coach travel. Sure, the railroads are needed. But you can't throw rails down everywhere. There's places a train can't go and a coach and team can."

"They don't see it that way, Ben."

"Tough. They're in for a fight."

"How do you plan to stop them?"

The big man took a moment or two to shift his weight on the buffalo robes. This operation was accompanied by a good bit of colorful profanity, but at last he was settled, and again reached for his drink. "There's just one thing holding that railroad up at this point. One thing in their way. I'm saying as far as the government giving them a go-ahead."

"Your stage line."

"Correct. See, Slocum, they've got enough shipping points for the southern herds—all through Kansas. Hardins Crossing don't need that. And most people don't want it. You know what it does to a town when it becomes a shipping center. Look at Abilene, Dodge, Ellsworth. Hell, people don't want to live like that anymore. You can't blame the trail men, but you can't blame the citizens either. Those boys are steaming for action when they come off that drive. Hell, you know how it is. But the citizens now are different. A lot of them go to church, want schools, and all like that. They're fed up with those bullyboys treeing their town, and busting up the cathouse every night and shooting all over the place. You know what I mean!"

"Times are changing," Slocum agreed. "But one thing doesn't change."

"What's that?"

"Money. Those drovers hot off the trail bring in a lot of money."

"I know, I know. I been there. I'm just telling you how it is in Hardins. Most people don't want anything to do with being a cattle point."

"But somebody does. Who?"

"Quince Dillingham, backed up by the Continental-Union outfit, that's who. Dillingham's been buying up land quick as he can. He's figuring on cleaning up. And some of the railroad men, too, of course. He's fronting for them, but he's mostly fronting for himself."

"Let me get it straight," Slocum said, leaning forward and holding the other man with his eyes. "This man Dillingham, plus Continental-Union, want the line, but as long as there's an operating stage running this route, Washington won't agree to it. That right?"

"Clear as a whistle. Why we're having all this goddamn trouble. They bust me and they can get permission to lay track." He took another long pull at his drink.

"What I'm saying is if the damn railroad was going to be a help to the country, I'd step aside, I'd even give 'em a boost. But hell, it's just a political candy. Somebody is getting rich. And by God it ain't gonna be at my expense!" His last words came out in a rush and were instantly followed by a coughing attack that turned him purple in the face, shook his huge frame, brought tears to his eyes, and thrashed the surrounding atmosphere with saliva. It was a long and, for an instant, to Slocum, a dubious moment. But Big Ben finally won his fight for control, though it cost him. He lay back, his body shaking with the effort he'd undergone.

Slocum waited.

Presently McCormack's voice spoke to the ceiling of the log cabin. "Shit, and shit again! The fuckin' croup is gonna bugger me if I ain't careful."

At this point Candida walked into the room, a worried look on her face. "Ben, I want you to stop talking now and get to rest." She turned to Slocum for support.

Slocum was already on his feet. "I'll leave him, Mrs. McCormack. He's got to rest."

A kind of gargle issued from the prone figure on the buffalo robes.

"We will accept no protest, Benjamin. Mr. Slocum is leaving you now," she said, raising her voice in emphasis to be sure he heard. She turned back to Slocum. "I'll show you where to bed down. I hope you'll be comfortable."

And for a moment her eyes caught his. "And please stop calling me Mrs. McCormack."

"My name is John," Slocum said. And he added, "Candy."

She had bent down and drawn a blanket over her husband, who was breathing heavily but more quietly now. When she straightened again her face was flushed, and to Slocum's astonishment he saw her hard nipples pushing against her dress like little fingers. The effort of tucking the blanket around McCormack's big body had made her slightly out of breath, and her hair had fallen down. She swept it back with her hand, and now to his even greater surprise he saw the dark purple birthmark on the left side of her face. He realized as she led him out of the room that all evening she had kept one side of her face averted, the arrangement of her hair helping as well to cover the birthmark.

It was the next morning—after a long and noisy sleep—that Big Ben announced they were all moving back to Hardins.

"Pulled out here so's I could take a look at things," he told Slocum over hotcakes and coffee, which the two women had prepared. "And also on account of till I get mended. I wasn't in no shape to stand off any moves from Dillingham's gunmen. I know they're his, though I can't prove it. The sonsofbitches threw down on Spicer and Biedler just outside the Pastime, and at the same time had 'em drygulched from the rear with Winchesters. Those two men had as much chance as a fart in a windstorm, let me tell you."

"Ben, calm yourself. You just mustn't get so excited." Candida turned to Slocum in appeal. "It isn't just his getting tromped by that horse, it's also his heart."

"Not a damn thing wrong with my heart!"

"Dr. Barney thinks otherwise, and I agree with him." Candida gestured toward Honey Mellody. "And Honey agrees with that, I know."

Honey was nodding her head vigorously. "Ben, you mind what Candy says. Doc Barney's a real Doc, not one of those blinkin' medicine hawkers."

This remark was greeted by a wave of a hand that resembled the paw of a grizzly, and very nearly knocked over the coffeepot as it swept aside anything that either of the women not only might have to say but might even think about Ben McCormack's condition.

"I know you likely figure I 'bout run my string out, but there's life here, let me tell you. By God, and that sonofabitch Dillingham is gonna find out!"

"Is it you and me, then?" Slocum asked, trying to get the subject away from the women. "Or have you got some more men?"

"I got half a dozen men. Not counting the men operating the stageline. Course by now, since I got tromped and bin laid up, who knows where they're lookin' for their pay. Like I told you, I come out here to study things a bit. See which way's best to go. You with me, Slocum?"

"Why do you think I came all the way out to this godforsaken place for?" Slocum asked.

A grin sprang into the big man's face, and, reaching over, he slapped Slocum on the arm. "Welcome! Welcome aboard, by God!"

John Slocum's words were etched with wry as he said, looking drolly at the women but speaking to Ben, "That arm you just patted so friendly-like happens to be the arm that took the bullet from those two bushwhackers."

And he turned his head and looked Big Ben McCormack right in each big eyeball.

He heard the sharp intake of Candy McCormack's breath, and at the same time the embarrassed laugh that died on Honey Mellody's lips.

A long pause followed, while, still without moving his eyes that were locked with McCormack's, Slocum lifted his coffee mug and drank.

"Then you'll be workin' for me," Big Ben said.

"No. I'll be working *with* you," Slocum said. And he stood up and walked out of the room.

He had told McCormack he would meet him in town. And even though he realized Hardins Crossing was no place for taking his ease, he still felt the need to work at the center of things. Besides, it wasn't likely—at least not yet—that anyone would try something with a lot of people about.

He decided he would be too tempting a target at the East-West house, and so with this in mind he rode back down to Hardins, planning to camp out. Taking his time, he reached his first view of the town at dusk. When he had ridden out to the North Fork the day before with Honey Mellody he had spotted a benchland near which flowed a creek lined with cottonwoods and box elders. And it was toward this particular area that he now guided the spotted pony.

He had checked his back trail carefully all the way from Ben's cabin. And now he scouted a wide circle around the benchland and even on the other side of the creek before he settled on where he would camp.

The flat place he finally picked was on a slight rise from where he could watch an approach from the town, while his rear was covered by the creek and the young cottonwoods and box elders. Finding a deadfall that would make a good protection in the event of an intruder, he laid out his bedroll.

In the soft breeze that had risen with the disappearance of the sun, he chewed on some beef jerky and drank cold coffee. He wasn't at all tired; sleep was no problem, but he wanted to think.

McCormack, he could see, was relentless as a grizzly. Slocum could tell the odds were overwhelmingly against the big man. Yet he would back him. Slocum enjoyed a good fight, knowing that one of the elements that made the difference between a good fight and a dull one was the odds. And anyway, Big Ben had offered him good pay.

McCormack was in a corner, largely due to the coming of the railroads, but also because of his injuring himself at such a bad moment, when Quince Dillingham had started his push for power. Laid low because of a wild bronc, not to mention a tricky heart, the man was all but out on his feet.

He had told Slocum he'd heard of him through Swede Byrner, but who Swede Byrner was—other than having heard from Hobe Winchy that he was the sheriff of Hardins—was a mystery to Slocum. Hell, he was thinking now, as he sat looking at the starry sky, a lot of lawmen knew him, or about him, but that was no recommendation. But he felt there was a mystery there, too. Why had a sheriff recommended him to McCormack, and who really was Swede Byrner? Slocum knew nobody by that name.

He continued to sit quietly, moving his position every now and again, just in case anybody was in the area and came snooping. Somehow, in some strange way, he and Big Ben McCormack had been thrown together. McCormack might be down, but Slocum knew he was a fighter. His offer had been a good one, and Slocum took him for a man of his word.

But the two women knew that Ben's heart wasn't as strong as it could be. Slocum realized that McCormack had been a lot more than just a high liver. The man had carried his body through all kinds of difficulties, not the least of which had been a long torture session with a notorious band of comancheros down in the Panhandle; whites disguised as Indians who warred, raped, murdered whoever and whatever their twisted instincts lighted on. Candida had told him some of these things when she'd come down to the barn, where he was saddling up to ride back to town. Then he'd watched her limping back to the cabin while McCormack's booming voice called for her, and he'd known one thing: that woman loved her man. She loved him enough to share him with another.

In his room at the widow Depone's boardinghouse, T. Wellington Throneberry sat on the edge of his bed engaged in one of his favorite pursuits. This was the careful perusal of his Grandine Catalogue, sometimes known as the Gambler's Bible, and in fact the source of the tools of his trade. The gambler's advantage tools, without which any card master who was serious in the pursuit of his craft would have been at a marked *dis*advantage, were numerous, and even awesome. The holdouts, shiners, trimmers, marked cards, blue glasses for "reading," and the cut dice that would roll tops or flats as needed almost never left the person of T. Wellington Throneberry. He carried these friends wherever he went in an elegant pigskin case with a brass clasp.

Practicing the techniques of his trade, and this included working with his advantage tools, had offered T. W. many a happy moment. As his uncle Obie had taught him: "You got to know it all, boy." Uncle Obie had been more than just a teacher, he had raised T. W. "from a button." That was a good spell ago, in T. W.'s memory, he being seventy going on eighty. And so, presently, as he sat in the widow Depone's boardinghouse, in his quiet room, practicing card cuts, second dealing, reading the backs of his marked decks with his blue-tinted glasses, and other refinements of the art, T. W.'s thoughts turned to his uncle.

Uncle Obie had been an educated man and demanding teacher when he took on the upbringing of his demised brother's boy. He had asked much from the youngster whom he took with him on the riverboats and later into the mining camps and cow towns.

T. W., just a shaver, had loved the riverboat life—those magnificent, stately vessels with their fabulous saloons, the ornate architecture, the always colorful clientele, sweeping grandly down the Mississippi. He had never gotten over his restlessness, his love of travel and adventure, nor had he ever wished to. Even so, he was surprised, at around the age of forty, to discover himself turning to another pursuit, and hiring on as a reporter for a newspaper in Denver. This was followed by a stint in San Francisco. Finally, at nearly seventy, to his outraged astonishment, he discovered his talents being called by the law.

The manner of his calling, however, had not been so exhilarating. Briefly, having been scissored by the minions of the law in Cheyenne over a dispute at cards which had ended with the demise of two players, T. W. had been persuaded to ply his talents in the way of rectitude with the offer of leniency, and possibly even forgiveness.

The offer didn't appeal to him in the least, but then neither did a stretch in the penitentiary, especially at his age. He told himself it was the best deal he could get, an axiom taught him by his uncle. "Boy, when you're holding the shitty end of the stick, let go fast, then cut your losses and get out of the game." Uncle Obie's "learning" had always been short, direct, right to the point, and unlike so much that passed professionally as "school teaching," it had proven useful.

In the present case, T. W. realized that the law, in the person of U. S. Marshal Cyrus Schultz, was resorting to the old dictum of "set a thief to catch a thief," which was all right with T. W. so long as it was clear that he was going to be let off.

His orders from the marshal and his deputy down in Cheyenne had been simple: "Find out everything you can about a man named Quince Dillingham, who is making his headquarters at Hardins Crossing."

T. W. had asked, "He a crook?"

"You tell me," Marshal Schultz had said, thus ending the conversation.

It had, of course, occurred to T. Wellington Throneberry that he, T. W., was only one of possibly several such "investigators." He felt, in fact, that he was being pulled into something big, and he was not at all happy about it. Yet he treasured his freedom. T. W. knew, as he knew nothing else, that were he to be sent to prison it would kill him. It would kill him dead.

Everyone had put a dollar into the six-handed game for a starter. T. W. had sighted the cold-decker the moment he started to deal. He was wearing a red vest, a striped shirt, and a derby hat squarely on top of his head. He was smoking a cheap cigar. But he was no greenhorn, that man. His hands were soft, his fingers clean, and clearly he did not earn his bread with pick and shovel or by riding the dust-choking drag behind a herd of bawling cattle. No, whatever mark he was going to make in the world would be at the gaming table.

T. W. had dropped into the Only Chance in the line of duty, that is, with the thought of catching the tone of the town. He was listening for the name "Quince Dillingham," but thus far he had not heard it. Meanwhile, he was enjoying his evening—not pressing the odds, just taking it easy so that he could stay quietly in the action without exciting unnecessary comment.

Seeing Banjo, the dealer, in action, T. W. knew he'd made a right choice. Nothing like a card game, or the dice either, for stretching people, flushing their weak spots. It wasn't always money that talked, his uncle Obie had told him, but the people who handled it.

Banjo was clean-shaven, save for his carefully trimmed mustache. His face was round, like a pudding, and his small hard eyes were like raisins. Tiny as his eyes were, T. W., an old hand at observation, could still see that they were filled with suspicion and theft. Banjo, he noted immediately, was swift as the wind with those cards, swift enough to easily slicker the bunch he was playing with.

The man on the dealer's left opened with a trey showing. The next man raised on a ten. T. W. caught another six, and on the following deal an ace. That gave him a pair of aces and a pair of sixes. Everyone had dropped out except Banjo, who had two kings and a trey showing.

It was at this point that T. W. felt a stirring in the big room and, looking up, saw a familiar face in the group watching the game. He was about to greet the man who had just walked in, but fortunately caught the look in John Slocum's eye and backed off. Obviously, "Mr. George Washington" didn't want to acknowledge any familiarity. T. W. was an old hand at such non-confrontations and easily shifted his attention elsewhere, just on the possibility that some predator might be watching. He knew that the man he was "investigating" was a power not only in Hardins, but in that whole part of the Wyoming Territory. And he took time to scold himself. It had been close. Was he slipping? Getting old? He felt something tighten inside himself but managed to let it go. Damn, but he had to keep loose. He'd stuck himself in this game to see what could be flushed, but he didn't want it to flush up his own rooty-tootie, to borrow from the lexicon of the Master, Uncle Obediah. His good humor restored, T. W. bent his attention to the game.

"Time to really sweeten the pot," Banjo, the dealer, was now saying, and his tiny eyes glittered.

T. W. watched, staying as close as the man's shadow, but without any overt sign of concern with anything other than his own cards. By now he was pretty sure Banjo was using a sleeve holdout. Banjo was no expert, but he had been fooling the others.

T. W. studied it, his brow bent to his cards, as though deciding what play to make. He knew he didn't have the cards to go against whatever Banjo was going to deal himself, and he also knew he sure wasn't going to get anything. He could fold, or he could stay in and watch the action. At the same time he was sure the big man with the green eyes and raven-black hair had caught it. For sure a man like that missed nothing. T. W. had never seen anything like that action on the stagecoach. The speed and the decision of it! Same with the action at the rooming house. And it was even contagious. He'd even moved faster himself when he'd shot the man coming in from the street. A long time since he'd shot anyone. By gosh, not bad for a seventy-going-on-eighty young feller!

Later, he realized it must have been the memory of that scene and the role he had played in the East-West that now prompted him—shoved him, really—to his present crazy action.

Banjo had just finished saying, "I'll bet it all," and pushed his whole pile of chips into the center of the table.

And then T. Wellington Throneberry heard himself say, "I'll see you." And he pushed his bet forward into the pot.

"God almighty," murmured someone behind him, and T. W's aquiline nostrils caught the strong smell of rotgut. At the same time that he felt the birds flying in his stomach, his chest, even in his loins, he was aware that the big man with the green eyes had shifted his stance.

Banjo was grinning. He had yellow teeth. "That's the way to play 'em, mister," he said. And he reached up and resettled his derby hat.

T. W. saw that the man was totally bald. But he knew now why he kept his derby hat on so much. Careless gamblers such as Banjo sooner or later gave themselves away. Some habit, a certain gesture, revealed everything to the discerning observer. T. Wellington Throneberry was a discerning observer. Indeed, he prided himself—justifiably so—on his skill. Banjo had decidedly revealed his giveaway.

"I'm right with you," T. W. said amiably. And he knew that the next card Banjo would deal him would be an ace or a six.

"Looks real pretty, don't she?" Banjo said, while he dealt T. W. a third six.

With an ace and three sixes showing and a second ace in the hole, T. W. had a full house, calling for a solid bet. This, of course, was what he knew Banjo was counting on. Banjo would without question deal himself a third king, the fourth being his hole card.

"Bet 'em an' play 'em," chuckled one of the onlookers.

When Banjo's forefinger touched the top card of the deck, T. Wellington Throneberry, with his heart closer to his throat than it ought to be, noticed that Slocum had inched his way closer to the dealer so that now he was standing right behind him.

Banjo reached up once again to adjust his derby hat, and then his hand dropped to deal the final card.

Quick as light Slocum reached down and grabbed the dealer by the wrist. With his other hand he reached into Banjo's sleeve and yanked the holdout into full view.

A shout went up from the group standing around the table.

"You sonofabitch!" screamed Banjo.

Slocum slammed the dealer's hand down on the table-top, and the fourth king dropped onto the chips.

It was like a dance, T. W. thought, as, immobilized himself, though only for a split second, Banjo's free hand streaked into his open coat. But Slocum was quicker. He grabbed the derby hat off the dealer's head and smashed him across the bridge of his nose with the hard brim.

Banjo fell back, screaming curses, with the blood pouring from his nose. Then Slocum chopped him in the Adam's apple with the hard edge of his hand.

The dealer dropped back into his chair and then sagged to the floor, gasping for air, his face covered with blood.

T. W., bristling with the excitement of the moment, released a long sigh and regarded the prone cardsharp. The room stood in quivering silence. The dance was over.

Sheriff Swede Byrner slowly swung his feet to the floor and sat up on the edge of his bed. He was just getting ready to stand up when his daughter entered the room—a pretty fair-haired girl of fifteen with a lot of freckles who ran the household since her mother had died.

"Dad, I thought we agreed you weren't going to try getting out of bed by yourself." Her tone, though admonishing, at the same time revealed that she was pleased with his activity. For too long she'd been worried. But his re-

covery was going well; so said Doc Barney, and so she
could see for herself.

"I ain't *trying* to get up out of this bed, I am *getting*
up," grumbled Cornelius "Swede" Byrner.

"I can see by your mood of light humor that you're
feeling better, sir," Sally Byrner said, her eyes teasing, and
leaning forward she gave him a peck on the cheek.

"By God, I told you, daughter, I sure ain't fixin' to die
in this goddamn town. Think of it! You die here in Hardins, you're a permanent resident forever! God almighty!"

She was laughing with pleasure at the return of his abra-
sive, grumbling battle with the world of Hardins Crossing.
Swede, a wiry man of small though dynamic stature, his
head covered with wild tufts of hair, stood yawning, then
stretched gently into the mid-morning smell of coffee and
baking-powder biscuits.

"Like to get myself outside some of your biscuits,
young lady." And as she reached out her hand to steady
him he brushed her away with a scowl. "Leave me be,
goddamn it; I was fighting bullets 'fore you ever saw the
light of day." He started out of the room.

She had to restrain her laughter, for he was wearing his
longhandles, and the trap door behind was hanging open
due to the missing button. She was about to mention that
she'd have to sew that, but thought better of it.

"Dad, you sit yerself down and I'll get you anything
you want."

"Whiskey wouldn't hurt."

"No whiskey. Dr. Barney said—"

"What does that old jackanapes know about anything!
Hell, the only reason for going to a man like that is so's
you know the best thing for you is to do the opposite of
what he tells ya! And that's a fact. I'll take some coffee;
and I'll get my own whiskey when I'm ready."

Suddenly, swift as a mouse, his mood changed. "Come here, you saucy thing, and give yer pa a nice hug. What's the matter? Sorry I didn't hop off, are you, leavin' you all my riches?"

"Daddy, I don't like you joking like that. Please don't."

"Sorry."

And she could see that he was.

While she poured his coffee and took the biscuits out of the oven she continued to talk. "Now, I know you don't want me to mother you, but please—for my sake—go slowly. This is your first day up. And you know Dr. Barney"— and she held up her hands, squeezing her face into exaggerated protest—"has told you, though he's an old fool, a rotten doctor, a pompous windbag, etcetera, etcetera, etcetera—that you must stay in bed longer. I'm not complaining, but I don't want to have to nurse you during the whole next year of my life." She took a deep breath and smiled fondly at him as he started to laugh but had to stop because of the pain. "Please . . . and that's all I have to say."

"By God, if you ain't a chip off the old block. Lucky your mother ain't here."

"Mom would never be able to stand two tyrants in the family."

When she sat down at the table across from him he said, "Anybody looking for me?"

"Anybody not would be an easier question to answer."

"Hobe, I reckon." He squinted against the steam coming from his cup of coffee as he raised it to drink. "Who else?"

"Hobe has been here a few times. And this morning a man named Slocum came. And of course a steady line of your friends on the town council."

She expected this last about the council to bring forth a

retort from her feisty father, but it was as though he hadn't heard her.

"Slocum, you say?"

"John Slocum. Do you know him? I didn't feel he was from hereabouts."

"No, he ain't—if it's the Slocum I'm thinking of. Big feller? Black hair?"

"And nice green eyes," Sally added with a small smile and a sigh. "He said he'd be back. Do you know him?"

"Maybe." He put down his coffee cup, then lifted it again, and now, leaning his elbows on the table, held the warm cup in both hands. "I reckon Hobe knows him. Bill Cooper gave me news on how Slocum busted up Hobe and two of his personal 'deputies' in the Only Chance. You hear about that?"

"No, I didn't. And I'm not interested in people beating up other people and all that. As you well know, Sheriff Byrner."

But Swede Byrner didn't pick up on his daughter's sashay into a much disputed zone—namely, his retiring and turning to a less active and less dangerous life. Swede Byrner's milky blue eyes were considering the news of his unexpected visitor as they gazed into the middle distance.

"Do you want me to let him in when he comes back?" Sally asked.

"No."

She looked at him, catching something different in his voice.

"Anything you want me to tell him?"

"Maybe you could get Hobe Winchy for me, Sal. But quiet-like. I don't want everybody in town knowing I'm up and about yet." He grinned at her suddenly as he saw the surprise in her face. "That's what you told me, didn't you—I mean, about a hundred times: to take it slow, not to go rushing back to work, and all that. So stop complaining."

Suddenly the girl stood up and came over to his side of the table and put her arms around his head. They stayed there like that for a long moment. Neither said a word. All that could be heard in the kitchen was the ticking of the clock standing by the galvanized washtub.

This time the doctor was in, but not his daughter. As Slocum walked into the small room that served Dr. Elihu Barney as his office, he wondered if the girl would appear. Then he remembered that she'd said she was getting married. Or had that been to put him off? Facing Dr. Barney now, he put her out of his mind.

"Just wanted to have you check this shoulder, Doctor," he said, realizing of course that it hadn't been his only purpose at all in coming to the office.

"Better get that shirt off," Doc Barney said.

He was a man in his middle years, steel-gray hair, a short beard, also steel-gray, and sharp gray eyes. Slocum saw no resemblance between him and his daughter until the doctor walked across the room, and, in a moment, the way his fingers touched around the wound.

"That's healing fine," Doc Barney said. "Just stay out of the way of any more flying lead and you'll likely make it to seventy or eighty, or—who knows?—longer." And a thoughtful smile entered his otherwise stern face.

"I'll do my best," Slocum said. He stood up and began pulling on his shirt. He was looking for an opening, but the doctor was putting away some of his equipment, evidently readying himself for some house calls. Slocum decided to simply confront him. "How's the sheriff doing, Doctor?"

Doc Barney was just closing his medical bag, into which he had put some bandages and a couple of bottles of medicine. He didn't look up. "You know the sheriff, do you? I'd say he was doing well." And he raised his eyes to look at his visitor.

"No, I don't say I know the sheriff, Doctor, but I heard about him getting shot up. And you may or may not have heard that I was in a mixup with his deputy just recently."

A sort of grin flashed through Barney's face. "Well, let's say I'd have been deaf, blind, and stupid not to have heard about that go-round. In case you're interested—and likely you're not—Hobe Winchy is also doing well. Though . . ." He paused, looking thoughtful as he dropped his eyes to the floor. "Though I suspect a number of citizens might wish otherwise. I guess what I'm saying, sir" —and he raised his eyes to look directly at Slocum—"I guess I'm saying good riddance to bad rubbish, though the varmint will likely be back. God knows why Swede Byrner ever picked him for deputy. Well"—he shrugged his shoulders, suddenly checked his fly to see if it was buttoned, and scratched himself behind his left ear—"I dunno. I hear you're a friend of Ben McCormack. If so, I'd advise you to watch your step."

The suddenness of the remark came as a surprise to Slocum, and he wondered whether he might have unleashed a possible torrent in the doctor. But he was disappointed, for Barney picked up his bag and started to the door.

Opening it, he stepped back and said, "After you, sir. And good luck to you."

Slocum waited on the boardwalk while Doc Barney locked his door. But the doctor said nothing more, and with a curt nod to his patient he made off down the street.

Slocum was wondering what Barney could have meant by his remark on McCormack when once again he heard the musical voice saying, "Are you looking for Dr. Barney, Mr. Slocum?"

And there she was, even prettier than before.

"Actually, I was hoping to run into you, Miss Barney, or . . . or is it 'Mrs.'?"

Her cheeks reddened somewhat at that, but she had herself in hand. "It's still 'Miss.'"

He must have shown his relief at that, for she said, "However, you never know what or when things are going to happen, do you?" She smiled.

Slocum actually felt her smile. There was nothing artificial about Jilly Barney.

"Would you join me for some dinner?" he asked.

"Thank you, but not right now." And with another smile, though one that was more formal, she took out her key and unlocked the door to her father's office.

Turning in the doorway she said, "I'm sorry if I seem unfriendly. I'm—well, I am what I am."

"Sure enough. So am I."

"I know. It's kind of you to ask me to dinner."

"I'll ask you again."

"You don't really know me," she said.

"You don't really know me either."

"Perhaps it's best to keep it that way."

"I don't think so. I think that would be real dumb."

But suddenly she was looking past him, and the expression on her face had changed. She dropped her eyes and, murmuring, "Excuse me," entered the office and closed the door behind her.

Slocum spun around, his eyes sweeping the street. But he saw nothing suspicious. Main Street at that time of day was crowded, and so he hadn't figured anyone would be a threat to him in that crowd. Not that a would-be assassin would worry over the niceties of killing an innocent bystander or two in the line of duty, but he'd have a hell of a time making a getaway.

Slocum saw nothing. As he started down the street, walking slowly, he kept looking at the people who passed by, wondering what the girl had seen, or who. But he had to give up on it. In any case, he did feel one thing strongly. He was sure she wanted to see him again.

7

With the many problems at hand—the looming confrontations with Print LeJeune, Hobe Winchy, maybe even with Banjo the crooked card mechanic, not to mention the building face-off between Big Ben McCormack and the railroad, plus whatever Sheriff Swede Byrner's attitude toward him might be—Slocum realized he was lucky to still be in one piece. Of course it was all connected. The attempted bushwhacking near Horse Gap, the stage holdup, the attack in the East-West were all part of a pattern; plus the provoked fight with Hobe Winchy. All this was linked with the fortunes of Big Ben McCormack. And Slocum remembered that Big Ben had heard of him through Swede Byrner. Who was Byrner? His daughter had said he couldn't see anybody right now. Doctor's orders. So he'd left his name. Anyway, unless the sheriff was about done for, he would have heard of Slocum's confrontation in town from his deputy. Sooner or later there would be some reaction from him.

Meanwhile, there was a major problem pressing in on him. He had no horse. After riding in from McCormack's North Fork camp, he'd decided to let prudence take over and had returned the spotted pony to the hitch rack near the East-West from where he'd taken it. It would have been too stupid to be seen with the animal, for he had stolen it, albeit from a would-be killer. Still, a horse was a horse, and in the West it was life. And so once again he was without a mount.

It still wasn't clear exactly what McCormack expected of him, for while they had discussed the ins and outs of the situation regarding the railroad scheme and Dillingham, Ben's sudden decision to get back to town had cut things short.

They had agreed to meet at the brick house, and at supper Slocum began by raising the subject of horseflesh.

"I've got a tough little buckskin you can have if you've a mind to," Big Ben said. "Good cow pony. Smart. Broke him myself. Keep him down at the livery, case of need. But you're welcome. Tell Cracker John, or I'll give you a note."

"I saw him. Fact, had my eye on him. Good enough," Slocum said, smiling. At least for the moment, his problem was solved.

"You can stable him down there, at my expense. John takes good care. See, I only get the best horseflesh; no sense in riding crowbait, not when you've got to get on and get out."

They both chuckled at that.

They had enjoyed a good meal cooked by Candida and were now savoring brandy and cigars in Ben's office. Honey had returned to her own quarters in town. She'd also gotten rid of the black mare, in the same way Slocum had done with his spotted mount. And so the three—Slocum, Ben, and Candy—had had a pleasant time together, though Slocum could tell that his host missed the lively Honey Mellody.

Then McCormack had shown him the house, the biggest and most notable in Hardins, though as Ben proudly pointed out, it was no match for any of his other mansions that he'd had built in various towns of the West. Still, it was what he now had. It was still a good deal better than most, was how Slocum looked at it.

McCormack held up his glass. "Well then, let's drink to our enterprise!"

Slocum followed suit, and the moment was a good one. "How long do you figure we have to hold out against Dillingham and Continental-Union?" he asked. "Do you see them as giving up? I don't."

"I don't either." Big Ben leaned forward, his whole body obviously behind what he was about to say. "The only way they'll give up is when they're smashed. Hell, it's the only way I'd give up!"

Slocum nodded, a grin starting on his face.

"Why do you ask?"

"Just wanted to be sure."

"Sure of me?"

"Sure of the play. See, I figure that deputy, Hobe, is working with Dillingham. That right?"

"I'd bet on it."

"But what about the sheriff?"

"I see what you mean. Swede's a mystery. I dunno. I know he don't give a shit for his deputy, but Hobe was all he could rustle up when there was the need. But Swede . . . I dunno. He come to Hardins maybe five years ago. Not much known about him, excepting he's a damn good lawman. Straight, tough, and you can't wangle him. Now, I know Dillingham has got to need him. You follow?"

"He's got to need him because he's the law, and Dillingham has got to appear to be with the law. After all, Continental-Union has to convince Washington that the line is needed." Slocum started to reach for his cigar, but instead decided to take a drink.

"You've got it. He needs Swede as a reliable witness that Continental is playing it straight."

"I wonder why Swede Byrner told you about me," Slocum said. "Are you close to him?"

McCormack leaned back and held up his hand to look at the back of it, obviously studying what his guest had asked him. "Reckon I shouldn't have put it like that. I don't discuss my business with Byrner, and I wouldn't want what I said then to go further than between us two."

"It won't. I got to know how I was spoken of, though. I never heard of Swede Byrner."

"Have you met him yet? I don't guess so."

Slocum shook his head.

"Even before I got racked up forking that bronc I was figuring I needed a ramrod for the stage line. A man can't do it all himself. But it had to be someone . . . well, let me put it this way—it's easy as hell gettin' somebody to help you, but it is like to impossible to get somebody to take something on."

"So you spoke to Byrner."

"Swede come by one of the stage stations where I was after we'd been held up again, and me and Dutch Zimmer shot our ways through. Swede come by to ask some questions. Hell, Slocum, he knew what was going on. Everybody did."

"But no proof on it."

"No proof on it." Big Ben took a slow pull at his drink.

He expelled his breath with a great whoosh. "By God, that there is good enough to raise a hard-on on a corpse!"

Slocum was grinning. He lifted his glass, but Big Ben had already reached for the bottle. He poured for both of them in silence.

Then Slocum lifted his glass again. "Here's to us, Ben. There are few like us—and few like us."

This brought a round of laughter from his host, who then fell into a coughing attack, but recovered just as the door opened and Candy McCormack came in, grave as a ghost.

"It's about time for some rest, wouldn't you say, Benjamin."

"I would not say so, madam. Now listen, I'd offer you a drink, but we-uns is talking business, so I reckon you got to skedaddle." And reaching out he gave her a friendly pat on the behind. And followed with a roar of merriment as she blushed, almost as dark as her birthmark. But there was laughter in her eyes as she left them, and, Slocum noted, a lively movement in her whole body, though she was still limping. He felt good for her, and he felt good about Ben.

But he suddenly thought of Honey Mellody, feeling the need for her, and so to quell his rising feeling he said, repeating himself, "So you spoke to Byrner."

Dragged back to the original subject matter, McCormack cleared his throat and put down his glass of brandy. "Just asked him if he knew of anybody in the country who might could handle a tough job. I reckon he knew what I was meaning."

"That's how my name came up. But how? How did he say it? See, I'm trying to place the man. If I know him, then he's got a different name now. Course, maybe I don't know him at all."

"He just said he only knew one man could cut that kind of job—I mean like he knew what I was talking about, you see—and that man was named Slocum. Didn't claim to know you. I asked, matter of fact, and he said no, he didn't know you; he'd heard of you; I didn't ask. No . . ." He paused, his dark eyes squinting into memory. "No, I didn't ask."

There followed a short silence, and then McCormack said, "Want to know something else, Slocum? Wells Fargo would like to buy me out. Fact is, they been my biggest competitor all along."

"Ever think of selling?"

"I had a plan once to work their price up—by topping them—and it worked for a while. They kept raising their offer. But . . . I dunno, I just didn't feel like it. Shit, I guess I'm ornery, like those women tell me."

And Slocum could do no more than grin at that.

After a moment when neither of them had said anything, Slocum stood up. "I'll be doubling the pressure, in any case," he said.

"You realize Dillingham's set you up as the target, least while I'm laid up—which goddamnit better not be for much longer. So Slocum, you save me some of it. I owe that sonofabitch a fistful."

"I'll leave you your share, McCormack. I owe the son-ofabitch a morsel or two myself."

It was a silver night, and the light of the thin moon touched the land in a way that could bring no comment, no thought, only a feeling.

Slocum felt it as he lay down on his bedroll by the deadfall where he had made camp. He had always preferred living outdoors, not only feeling the freedom and mobility of such a way of life but also appreciating the difference and, at the same time, the connection with the day and night, the night and day. What he liked especially on such a night as this was the smells. And the way a man could feel his way in the darkness, which, as now, was for him nearly as clear as daylight.

As a result of his years on the trail, John Slocum's perceptions were as keen as an Indian's. Possibly this was a consequence of his Cherokee blood strain, but also it was due to the way he had lived. His eyesight, his keenness of hearing, and maybe especially his sense of smell had more than a few times alerted him to danger.

He had just stretched out on top of his bedding when he smelled her. A perfume that he wasn't familiar with, and it wasn't at all heavy yet it came to him. And then he heard her.

Then, as he was almost seeing her, a cloud darkened the sky and he could make out only her vague shape.

"I'm over here," he said, and already his organ was eagerly anticipating Honey Mellody's soft, resilient, and most eager body.

In the next moment she was in his arms and they were each pulling off the other's clothing.

"I thought you'd never get here," Slocum said, and he realized something was different.

"It's not Honey," she said, as she stood next to him suddenly without moving. "It's . . . it's Candy."

"Let's get the rest of your clothes off then," Slocum said. "And we can lie down."

Quince Dillingham had been not only surprised but alarmed to see Jilly Barney and the man he'd been told was Slocum together outside Doc Barney's office. And for a moment he had experienced the searing wire of jealousy pulling through his body. But Dillingham's mind was his strongest asset, and he turned to his thoughts instantly for relief, telling himself that the meeting must have been a result of a visit to the doctor. And in fact, shortly after the moment he had checked with one of his spotters and learned that indeed Slocum had been in the office and had accidentally run into the girl just as he was leaving. This somewhat relieved his jealousy and anger at the girl's sudden decision not to marry him.

Quince Dillingham, as he saw himself, was decidedly not the sort of man anyone rejected. Anyone! However, the game wasn't over. He would continue to woo her, and at the same time put pressure where it would do the most good. For instance, there was Doc Barney's trouble over water rights with his neighbors out at Betty Creek. It had been his entry in the first place with Jilly, and it could be again.

At the same time, there was the question of this man Slocum. And now, having returned to his office, he addressed this question to the man standing before his desk.

"Well, I can't say that you've exactly filled your assignment, Winchy. I see that Slocum is alive and hale and hearty, and even enjoying the society of an attractive lady in full view of the citizens of Hardins Crossing. You failed completely—or your men did—at the East-West. Not to mention the stupid play you tried to make in the Only Chance."

"Mr. Dillingham, I know I done wrong in the saloon. And I already told you I just thought I was following orders, to try to backwater him."

"You're lying. First of all, your conversation was overheard. And I know you were trying to line your pocket not only at the expense of the law—and who cares about that? —but at mine. At *my* expense! You fool. And you can even *think* of handling a man like Slocum! You fool! You goddamn bloody fool!"

To the beleaguered Hobe Winchy, Quince Dillingham's harsh words were as painful as John Slocum's blows. He felt as though he'd been horsewhipped, tarred and feathered, strung up with wet leather and left while it dried and tightened around his wrists, his ankles, his neck.

A long moment filled the room as Hobe stood there, his thoughts scattering through his head like mice looking for a place to hide.

Dillingham leaned forward with his elbows on his desk, his fingertips together forming an arch. His head was raised slightly so that his two forefingers touched his bottom lip, while his eyes were dead center on Hobe Winchy.

"What is the condition of Swede Byrner? I had heard he was recovering, but that was two days ago. Tell me the latest."

Relief flooded through the man standing on the other side of the desk, and he spoke swiftly, "Swede's doing fine. He'll be up and about anytime now."

Hobe wisely did not add anything about the sheriff's tearing him apart for his behavior in the Only Chance with John Slocum.

He didn't have to. Quince Dillingham had that figured out. He knew the caliber of Swede Byrner. Indeed, a linchpin of his major plan was the character of the sheriff. Those roistering fools from the Double Bar outfit had come within a whisker of upsetting that when they'd tried to shoot up the town and Byrner had stopped them—and almost been killed in the process. Close. The man was alive, and shortly he would be active. That meant he was available to be handled—manipulated. Because it was essential to have the law on his side. After all, there was still that dodger on Slocum. His people in Cheyenne had printed a number of them. It was just possible that Byrner might not check on them right away, might not catch on to their being fake, that he might even take Winchy's word for it that they were the real thing.

"Did Byrner mention the dodger on Slocum?"

"No, he don't even know about it. You want me to show it to him?"

"No, let him find it. And then if he asks about it you say you sent a message to Cheyenne to check on it. Say that before he can come at you with it."

"It looks one hundred percent real. Why get him suspicious?"

"Because, you fool, he may know that McCormack sent for Slocum, and by now he certainly knows the trouble that gentleman has been having, not only at Horse Gap with those two fools who bungled, but also the episode on the stage, and finally those idiots who bungled everything at the East-West House. Knowing that, and how Slocum handled things, he might just question that dodger. And it would be a whole lot better if you give the impression that you yourself questioned it. It will put you ahead. Also, it will all take time."

"But what then if Swede finds out it's a fake? He'll still come at me about it?" Hobe was beginning to sweat at the complication. He liked his thoughts to be straight, and not only was subtlety something well beyond him, but whenever it appeared—as it often did with Dillingham—it was a sore threat.

Quince Dillingham lowered his hands, leaned back in his chair, and crossed his legs, keeping his eyes still on Hobe Winchy.

"You will tell him that you sent a message to Cheyenne to check on the authenticity of the wanted notice. Should Byrner question why no reply has come back, you will simply say you don't know. Maybe the message you sent got lost, stolen, whatever. But time will have passed. And get this—Byrner will wonder. He will wonder what is going on. He will begin to feel surrounded, in a way. You understand me? He won't know what's happening, but he will begin to feel outnumbered, outgamed, and he could begin to worry. In a word, he'll be where I want him. Now, that's enough. You can go."

And he leaned forward and picked up a paper from his desk and began reading it.

Hobe Winchy had no problem with the subtlety of this moment. He could figure that the meeting was ended.

"You understand, LeJeune, that McCormack's Cheyenne run has got to fail. Those stages must not get through without some sort of trouble. But not to overdo it."

Print LeJeune nodded. "I got'cha, Mr. Dillingham."

"Sit down."

If Print LeJeune had been gifted with even a slightly higher intelligence he would have realized that this gesture alone indicated the gravity of the situation Quince Dillingham was discussing.

"I know that McCormack—especially in view of the fact that he's been injured—will be getting Slocum to manage his stage runs. I know that's why he called on him in the first place. Slocum might even be riding shotgun himself."

"That's fine with me. I got plenty to get even with that feller."

"I don't care what you do, I want that line to collapse. Do you understand what I'm telling you?"

"I do. You want that line busted."

"But with no suspicion on us. You must not allow it to get out of hand."

"All right, then. And what about Byrner?"

"I'll take care of Byrner."

Dillingham rose to his feet. He was taller than the man on the other side of the desk, and he seemed even taller than he actually was by the way he looked down his long nose at Print LeJeune.

"That will be all, LeJeune. Just remember that I'm depending on you. Don't disappoint me. Oh, and LeJeune, we'll have a, uh, someone coming out to assist our operation. I expect you to cooperate with him fully."

Print had stopped at the door and turned as his boss spoke. A tight look came into his face as Dillingham concluded what he had to say.

"This feller got a name?"

There was a very thin smile on Quince Dillingham's mouth and in his eyes as he said, "O'Hagen," he said. "Manuel, I believe. Yes. Manuel O'Hagen." And he watched carefully to see how Print LeJeune took it.

Print LeJeune left the office with Dillingham's last words vibrating in his ears.

Behind him Quince Dillingham closed his front door, then returned to his office and sat down at his desk.

The conversations and instructions with Hobe Winchy and Print LeJeune had been conducted with other men as well. Men of similar talent—swift with guns, fists, loyal to their master, with no scruples, and with closed mouths.

For the man who was planning to run the Continental-Union rails through Hardins Crossing and on east had received word that the destruction of McCormack's stage line had to be accomplished quickly. For as long as the line was in good operation, the men in Washington had informed him, a sale to Wells Fargo could be expected. This event would give McCormack a lot of money that he might decide to use to compete for the other end of the line—from

Cheyenne east to St. Joe. The man was not the sort in any case to sit still. And with Slocum running his operation, he might do anything. Dillingham had a full report on John Slocum, and he had no illusions about him.

But the essential point was not to lose Hardins. To hell with Continental-Union if need be. Dillingham had to have Hardins as a shipping point for the Texas beef market—for himself.

Slocum, yes—but Swede Byrner had to be taken care of as well, though in a different way, for he needed the approval of the law. And now suddenly having discovered Swede Byrner's past, which the sheriff had so far kept so well to himself, Dillingham knew that Byrner had to be the man to "understand" his position. In a word, the sheriff could be manipulated. And would be. All along he had been wondering how would be the best way to manipulate Swede Byrner, but out of the blue Manny O'Hagen had handed him the answer.

And yet for all his concern over his plan, Quince Dillingham was finding trouble at this particular moment in keeping his mind on business. In spite of everything—the gravity of the situation, the need for careful planning and for quick action—he nevertheless found his thoughts returning again and again to Jilly Barney.

Yes, he could see where he'd made his mistake. He had taken her for granted, he hadn't romanced her sufficiently, he had simply assumed that she would marry him, especially after he had spoken to her father about buying up his property south of Betty Creek, and so helping him out of his problem with his neighbors and water rights.

All the same, he reasoned, he was indeed a special catch for such a girl—for any young woman. He was. No question about it. He was handsome, rich, energetic, puissant (he liked that word), enterprising, and powerful and mysterious. What else could a young woman want? And he had a string of conquests to his credit!

Still and all, it had to be admitted he had rushed things. Well, he would go slow now. She was just shy, immature, afraid perhaps of his great force. He recalled just how she had said yes to his proposal. It had been rather an automatic response. "I'd like to consider that." Those were her exact words. And he had simply taken that for a vow of devotion.

He had been extraordinarily circumspect in his behavior. He had made no brash advances, had in fact only kissed her half a dozen times, and nothing more. A squeeze or two, but not in any major area, had been all he'd tried. He'd been so careful! After all, it wasn't just the marriage; there was Doc Barney's acreage. He wasn't just proposing to Jilly Barney. In a manner of speaking the proposal had to be to Dr. Barney too. Well, by damn, the good doctor would certainly see what a fine son-in-law he'd had the good fortune to acquire!

He had to admit, though, that her suddenly breaking off the engagement—which had only been on for a couple of weeks—had spurred his appetite for her the more. Even now, just thinking about her he found his erection a torture in his tight pants. Thank God he was seeing Stella. He looked at his pocket watch, and at that very moment there came a knock at the door. God, what luck!

He made himself go slowly to answer the door. Let her wait a bit, even worry whether he might have forgotten their appointment. The knock came again, and he carefully opened the door.

A tall man with broad shoulders, wearing a holstered pistol, confronted him. "Your name Dillingham?"

The shock that ran through him when he found out it wasn't Stella at the door almost made him stammer. Yet he recovered. In his field of intrigue, bullying, cheating, and inciting others to violence on his behalf, Quince Dillingham was a professional. He rallied and recovered all in the span of a breath or two.

"Who wants to know?" Though he knew full well.

"I'm Slocum. I want to talk to you." And he pushed his way through the door. If Dillingham hadn't stepped aside, he would have crashed into him.

"I'm busy. Now get out of here or I'll call up some of my men." Dillingham had unbuttoned his coat as he saw Slocum's hand move slightly toward his six-gun.

"Easy does it, Dillingham. Don't try me. I'll cut you down before you can even touch that hideout."

"What do you want?"

This was not the scene Quince Dillingham had imagined. For once he was not in charge. Somehow Slocum had gotten the upper hand, and for the moment he didn't know how to handle it.

But Slocum was taking his time. "I'm here to tell you something, Dillingham." His eyes bore into the other man's. "You likely know I'm running Ben McCormack's stage line to Cheyenne. I'll have men on the stages who will shoot to kill anyone who tries to stop them. I want you to hear that. Not only will my men and I retaliate on your men if they try to stop the stage, but I personally will retaliate on you. Do you understand me?"

Slocum stood squarely in front of Quince Dillingham, his eyes like chips of green stone. But he could also feel the other man's hardness and knew that Dillingham was not going to be an easy mark. It was why he had chosen to hit hard, and first, carrying the fight to Dillingham.

The next words that Quince Dillingham spoke offered firm evidence of his position. "Go fuck yourself, Slocum," he said in a bored tone of voice.

A hard grin came into John Slocum's face. "I've had two of your men try to drygulch me. I know you were behind that, and also the bunch that tried to get me at the East-West, which means you've got Winchy and his boys on your payroll. Now I'm just warning you—this time. Anything happens—get me, anything—I'm not going to look to prove it, I'll come for you."

Slocum held the other man's eyes long enough for his words to dig in, and then he turned and walked back out of the house.

Dillingham stood in the doorway watching the big man walking away. The house was at one end of Main Street, and Slocum was walking in the general direction of a prospector's box wagon with a dun-colored old crowbait standing between the shafts only a few yards away.

Dillingham watched him, watched his back. The damn fool, he was thinking, offering himself like that. What arrogance! What contempt! Only he himself could pull off something like that—walking away with his back exposed like that. A perfect target.

Too late he realized even his thought was a mistake. As his hand moved, without himself realizing it, Slocum spun, and in less than a wink Quince Dillingham was facing the hard round barrel of the big Colt .44.

"Don't even think of drawing on me, Dillingham. I thought we covered that already."

"I must say you're pretty fast there, Slocum." Dillingham's smile was not as easy as he would have liked, but it was there. He dropped his hand slowly to his side; astounded at what he might have done. Then, without another word he turned and walked back into his house and closed the door.

Later, at the Only Chance, big Ben McCormack said,

"Slocum, for a minute there I thought my signal wasn't clear."

"Clear as mud, Ben."

"But I signaled you were in the clear. You didn't see it?"

"Not any more than Dillingham did. You set yourself and that wagon so the sun was not only in Dillingham's eyes but in mine, too, for Christ sake. He couldn't see you, but neither could I."

"Jesus! Then how did you know he was going for his gun?"

"Actually, he wasn't. He was thinking pretty hard about it, though."

Big Ben McCormack stared at him in astonishment, his jaw dropping. "Holy shit," he said, and reached for his chewing tobacco. "Holy shit!"

8

"Hyah! Giddop! Giddop!" The long leather snaked out and cracked like a rifle shot over the heads of the lead team. And again cracked, as the driver, half out of his seat, swore at the horses. The thorough braces creaked wildly and the sweating teams lunged flat out as they entered the canyon. Behind the coach dust rose in blinding clouds as the iron tires screamed on the rocky road.

Immediately ahead the road made a sharp bend between two jutting faces of rock. The youthful driver pulled on his lines to slow the coach so it could make the turn. Then he saw the men signaling him to stop.

"I wanna make a run for it, goddamn it," he snarled at the guard seated beside him.

"Better not. Lookey there! Christ, they're all over the place!"

"I'm gonna run fer it. We got a chance!"

"Slocum said no. Remember? He told us to stop if we got braced."

In time, as a warning shot rang out, the driver came to his senses, remembering their instructions—that if they were held up they were to submit and offer no resistance.

Cursing, mumbling to himself about the stupidity and weakness of such orders, the young man pulled his team to a halt. His name was Billy Wagner, and he had just turned twenty-one. His companion, the guard, was a man of thirty-five. Harvey Fletcher was an old hand at riding shotgun.

A shout rose from one of the passengers inside the coach as in a thick cloud of dust the coach all but crashed to a halt behind the steaming, trembling horses.

"Everybody out! Just do what you're told and you won't get hurt!"

The man issuing the orders was riding a steel-gray horse, a tight little cow pony who looked like he'd worked cattle. The passengers began to step down from the coach.

Two masked men suddenly popped out into the road now, their six-guns aimed at the pair seated on the box.

"Driver, you git down here and unhitch these teams. And you—" he pointed his gun at the guard—"you throw down the money sack. Hurry it!"

"There's no money on board this trip," the guard said. "Just got the mail sack."

"Throw it down, I said!"

"Listen," Fletcher said. "A sack of money was supposed to come with us today, but for some reason or other they didn't load it on. There's nothing here. I swear it."

"Me too," added Billy Wagner, the driver. "You can take a look for yourself." And without further ado, he stood up on the box and, reaching to the roof of the coach, pulled down the sack of mail and dropped it at the road agents' feet.

Three more masked men suddenly appeared out of the bushes lining the road.

"Open the sack," one of them said to Billy Wagner.

The boy shrugged and jumped down and began to untie the sack.

The passengers, badly frightened, were now told to line up at the side of the road, and the driver and guard were ordered to join them.

All were searched quickly and gave up money, gold watches, rings, a diamond stickpin. The road agents searched the stage but could find no money sack. They rifled the mail pouch, but it was hardly worth the trouble. Finally they ordered the passengers back into the coach, then told the driver to hitch the teams and get going.

As the stage pulled out and gathered speed, the passengers broke into a gabbling of relief at having escaped so easily.

But up on the box the driver was arguing with the guard. "I could have whipped 'em on through and outrun those sonsofbitches, damn it!"

"That ain't the orders we had, young feller," the guard said. "Lemme tell you, a feller like that Slocum feller, a man don't argue with him when he's giving the orders. He had some reason for telling us like he did."

"I'll believe that when I see it," young Billy Wagner said, arguing it to the bitter end.

"Shut up!" Fletcher suddenly snapped. "Hear that!"

"Sounds like gunfire."

"That it is. And it's coming from back in that canyon where we was, by jingo!" Harvey Fletcher suddenly let out a hoot of laughter. "By jingo, I'll bet that Slocum feller has spoked 'em right up their ass!"

The day broke hot, with clouds already forming along the eastern horizon.

"She's fixing to rain," Swede Byrner said to his daughter as he returned from his study of the morning sky and settled down to hotcakes and coffee.

Sally looked at him across the table. "You'll be all right today, then?" She had made her voice casual, or so she thought, certain as any fifteen-year-old that she was fooling him.

"Young lady, I'm fine. Now stop that silly worrying and nattering over me. Damn it . . . I mean, by golly, I was handling myself 'fore you was even thought of."

The caliber of his raspy retort immediately informed her that he was indeed all right. It was what she had wanted to know in the first place, but, still with the special intelligence of her new years, she understood for certain that he was about back to normal. And she felt happy.

"Are you going to see that man Slocum?" she asked.

"Why you want to know?" Holding a piece of hotcake in his fingers, he cleaned up the last of the syrup from his plate. And popping the delicious morsel into his already crowded mouth he cocked an eye at her.

Under his inspection Sally felt her face reddening, and so she lowered her head and pretended to cough.

Swede Byrner wasn't fooled. And he didn't mind. A man such as Slocum had to attract hero-worship, and female admirers, of any age. What did bother him was something quite else. But suddenly he was attacked by an itch in his crotch and, leaning forward, he surreptitiously scratched himself. Relieved, he smiled inside, realizing how alike they were—she with her cough covering her embarrassment, himself leaning forward to hide his scratching. But he didn't dally with this reflection. Sheriff Swede Byrner was back in business this day.

"I told you I didn't want you taking up guns," he said, coming flat out with it.

And this time there was no hiding for either of them. Father and daughter faced each other across the table in a silence that seemed to shake with the echo of his hard words.

"How did you find out?" she asked.

"Smelled it. Got a nose like a grizzly. Always had. And I know my own daughter, damn it." He studied her. "I'm telling you again—there's one gun in this family, and one only. And that's me."

"I wanted to help you."

"'Preciate that. I do. But at the same time, I don't appreciate your getting yourself shot up, which by God is what's gonna happen to you more sooner than later if you don't stop."

"But you've got no one to help you," she insisted. "And you've been laid up. I felt I had to."

He watched her fighting back the tears.

"I've got my deputy."

"Hobe Winchy! But he's a—a nothing. You've told me he's dishonest, and that he hangs around with a really tough bunch of saddle bums. What has he done to help you?"

He leaned forward, scratching again beneath the table, but still with his attention fully on what he was going to say. "I'll tell you. Hobe serves a good purpose. As long as Quince Dillingham thinks I don't know Hobe's actually working for him and his railroad bunch, then I got time to see what I can do."

"But what are you going to do? Mr. McCormack's a decent man, but you've told me Mr. Dillingham wants to get rid of him. Something like that. I don't even want to think about what you mean by 'get rid of him.'"

"Dillingham wants to run track through to St. Joe, by way of Cheyenne. That means he's first got to get rid of McCormack's stage line; otherwise the men in Washington won't make the agreement. It's that simple. And not so by-the-way, he also wants to take over Hardins Crossing." He sniffed, "Course, far as I'm concerned he's welcome to the place. Exceptin', not on his terms, I better say also."

"But if you get in their way . . ."

"I won't. Dillingham figures he can diddle me. Shucks, I'm just an old country boy. Let him diddle." He stood up. "I got my eye on other things besides that rapscallion."

"What?" she asked, only slightly mollifed as she stood up and came toward him.

"On me cute, smart, lovely, pain-in-the-neck daughter," he said.

Then, with a big sniff, all the way through his wide nose, he picked up his hat and departed. "I'll be in my office," he said over his shoulder.

It was early. Across the deserted street Heavy Tom Swoboda staggered along the boardwalk. As usual Heavy Tom was drunk with trail whiskey. Somehow he always managed to walk, or at any rate stagger, to the livery, where, in the loft, bedded in hay, he would sleep his way toward his next bout with the booze.

Sheriff Byrner took him in as they passed each other, with the street between them. A good while back Swede had hired Heavy as a deputy, back in the days when he didn't drink so much. But on his first assignment Heavy had taken on more fuel than was necessary and, firing at a departing thief as he escaped from the Red Rose Cafe, had missed him and instead destroyed the cash register inside the eating establishment. The irate owner had demanded payment, and finally got it. But that ended Heavy Tom's career as a lawman.

The pickings as far as deputies went around Hardins had never been good. Swede's predecessor, Cal Joyner, now residing in Hardins' "permanent hotel" just outside town, had had the same trouble getting men to help the law.

Yes, for sure, Sally had her gripe. He understood it and agreed with her, though never saying as much. But he was here in Hardins for a purpose. The problem now was that he wasn't any too sure but that with all the action that had been stirred up somebody might find out about it.

T. Wellington Throneberry stood at the corner of Main and the alley that led past the Hello Cafe and surveyed the morning passersby. So far he had not dug up any important information for Marshal Cyrus Schultz down in Cheyenne. He had seen Quince Dillingham passing in the street, he had made discreet inquiries in all the usual places—the barber, the saloon, the cribs—but nothing of singular importance had appeared.

T. W. was beginning to be slightly concerned over his lack of material to send to Cheyenne. He was not the sort to worry unduly, but he had felt the need coming from Marshal Schultz when he had assigned him to the task. It was no small thing.

He had noted that Dillingham was never far from one of his hired gunmen and that he enjoyed the company of two attractive ladies—Doc Barney's daughter, Jilly, and the redhead who visited his home at varied hours of the day and night and remained for an indecent length of time, but not overnight. And he had heard gossip that Dillingham was trying to take over the town, pack the council, turn people against Ben McCormack.

But no vital information was forthcoming—nothing that would earn his release from Schultz's hard grip. Damn it! There had to be something. From long experience—not to forget Uncle Obediah's instruction not only in cards and dice and gambling in general but also in the art of living— T. W. knew that the real knowledge lay in people's behavior: the way they did things much more than what they did. In the unsaid word, the avoided look, the throwaway gesture. In short, from the unexpected.

And yet he was totally unprepared for the totally unexpected when it finally did happen.

It was early morning.

"Terwilliger." The voice, coming from behind, caught him as, with the tip of his tongue, he was trying to pry a piece of his breakfast from between two back teeth. And T. W. Throneberry didn't have to turn around to see who it was who had addressed him by his almost wholly unknown first name.

"There's no one around close, you can turn."

T. W. managed to turn quite easily to face the tall, thick-bodied man in the tight clothes with the tied-down Colts, one at each thigh.

"Surprised, are you?"

"Yes, I am. I thought you—"

"You thought I was in the pen."

T. W. nodded. "Good to see you, Manny."

"No, it isn't. You're scared shitless, you old fuck! But get this—there ain't nobody here knows me. Exceptin' you. You know two things about me. You know my name. And the second thing you know is that if you tell anybody

I'm here and who I am I'll kill you. I'll kill you in pieces. Do you get me?"

"Yes. Yes, I get you." To T. W.'s astonishment he realized that he was not shaking, he was not terrified or even sweating. And he should have been. Manuel O'Hagen was positively the last person in the whole West he would ever have wanted to see again. He had been sure he was safe in Folsom, but he must have escaped.

It was eerie. It was as though O'Hagen was reading his mind. "I busted out," he said. "I've been watching you for the past hour. I know just how I'll kill you if you spill on me. Why I approached you, get it. Didn't want you to see me, to spot me and then go tattle-taling to John Slocum."

A grin suddenly appeared on O'Hagen's face, and since he had eyeteeth that were both prominent and came to sharp points, it give him the look of a hungry and very wicked wolf. At any rate, that was how T. W. saw it. Yet he was still not shaking.

"So what can I do for you, Manny?"

"No names."

"So what can I do for you?"

"Still got that snotty way with you, don't you?"

T. W. said nothing.

"Where's Slocum?"

"I don't know."

"Cut it out, Terwilliger."

"I mean, I don't know where he's at right now. He was in town, then he disappeared. Now? He could be back. It's early in the day."

T. W. could see that O'Hagen wasn't completely satisfied. He was weighing his reply for sincerity. Apparently, he decided that it was the truth.

"Want you to do something for me, Terwilliger."

"I can guess what it is," T. W. replied sourly.

O'Hagen grinned his wolf grin. "Always said you was a bright one."

"What d'you want?"

"I want you to tell me Slocum's moves."

"Where can I find you?"

"I'll find you. And remember—don't even think of crossing me. I know where the body's going to be buried, if you forget my instructions."

And he was gone.

T. W. found that, yes, now he was sweating.

At the same time he discovered another emotion was riding him. More than just about anything he could think of, he hated being called "Terwilliger."

The man with the thick body had narrow shoulders, and it was this physical aspect that caught Sheriff Swede Byrner's attention as he stood looking out of his office window. In fact, the moment he saw the figure across the street, from the back, he knew who it was. Only one man he'd ever seen had a build like that. And now, as though to prove it, the tall stranger turned and stood there on the opposite boardwalk, as though looking for something. Swede knew what he was looking for. But at that same moment there was a knocking at the back door of his office, the little door that led outside toward the outhouse.

Turning quickly, the sheriff drew back from the window, locked his front door, and then stepped quickly to the door at the back, where someone was still knocking.

It was no surprise to the sheriff to see that his visitor was T. W. Throneberry. He opened the door and locked it behind his visitor, neither of them speaking. They moved into the room that served as the sheriff's office and sat down.

When Throneberry started to speak, Swede cut him off.

"I know," he said. "I saw him through the window."

"Sheriff, he must not know I'm here. I have to tell you that right off. But I want you to know I'm doing my job. I've got a strong notion O'Hagen's here on account of Dillingham."

Swede Byrner had cut himself a thick chew of tobacco while T. W. was talking, and now he popped it into his mouth, taking the chew right off the razor-sharp blade of his skinning knife—to T. W.'s astonishment and concern, for he was sure the sheriff was about to cut off his own nose.

"I'll get the news to Schultz pronto," Swede Byrner said. "Now, you better get out of here. I expect him any minute." And he nodded in the direction of the street.

And to emphasize his point there came a loud push at the locked door, followed by a severe knocking.

T. W.—seventy going on eighty, no matter—was out of that office lickety-split. And as he hurried through the back of town away from the danger that had so suddenly appeared in his life, he discovered that now he was indeed shaking, at least some, at the prospect of confronting the anger of Manny O'Hagen, or the hard resolve of Sheriff Swede Byrner, or the ultimatum of Marshal Schultz. By God, he was caught between hellfire and damnation. He was surrounded, and if he wasn't damn careful he'd be consumed. By the law and the outlaw. Yes, indeedy, Uncle Obie had warned him. "Life is dangerous," he'd said, and then added, "But if it don't kill you, it keeps you young."

A gingery view of the situation, T. W. reflected as he hurried toward the far end of town. Now, as he began to relax a little and his breath slowed, he turned to look behind while crossing somebody's backyard. The next thing he knew his neck felt as though it had been broken and he was lying flat on his back looking up at the bouncing clothesline that had nearly garroted him.

"Mindfulness," Uncle Obediah had instructed. The word of the master swept in, and he was filled with shame at his stupidity at not looking where he was going. But, of course, it could be taken as a useful warning. Clinging to that piece of a small thought, T. W. rose, brushed off his clothes hurriedly, and now proceeded at a slower, more careful pace. A drink, a couple of hands of cards, perhaps he would treat himself to an expensive cigar. For—by damn!—surely he had made restitution to Marshal Schultz and the law in what he had just gone through this day!

The sheriff of Hardins Crossing and his visitor stood facing each other.

"Been a long time," Manuel O'Hagen said easily, with his thumbs hooked into his loaded belt.

"Not long enough."

"You ordering me out of town, Mulligan?"

"The name is Byrner. Sheriff Byrner."

"But still Cornelius?"

"I am not ordering you out of town—for the moment, O'Hagen. That means I will have my eye on you. The first funny move you make, I'll be coming for you. Now git!"

A crafty look came into O'Hagen's face. Something was puzzling him. "Don't you want to know why I'm here in Hardins? Or how I got out of the pen?"

"I know how you got out of the pen. I got sent dodgers on you."

"And then, you know why I'm here?"

"I'll sure enough find out."

"I think you will, Cornelius." He had half turned toward the door. "I think you will." And suddenly one of those big six-guns was in his hand. "See, prison didn't hurt my draw that much." He grinned. "How's yours, I mean since you took all that lead. I heard about it." The grin tightened. "But then I was always faster'n you, Cornelius."

"And I was always more accurate than you, you dumb bell."

"Remember I knew you when, Cornelius. You got a tin star now. These people here know you're Corn Mulligan, the once-famous outlaw?" He suddenly dropped his six-gun back into its holster. "I don't reckon so. But maybe one or two might be interested to hear about it. Just remember that." And with an abrupt nod, the tall, thickset man with the narrow shoulders and twin six-guns opened the door and stepped out into the street.

When the door had closed Swede took off his hat, ran his forearm across his forehead, and then spat—accurately —into the spittoon by his desk. Then he sat down, tilted his chair back onto its hind legs, placed his hat forward so that his eyes were covered from the daylight coming in, and folded his hands together across his belt buckle.

Through a small opening that had been especially cut for the purpose at the back of the building came a black-and-white shepherd dog. His name was Tip, probably because the end of his bushy tail was white. He walked into the front room and surveyed his master, the sheriff, listened to the snores rolling down his nose, yawned, and then, coming closer to the man asleep in the chair, he lay down, placed his long jaw on one of his forearms, and closed his eyes. In a moment or so Tip had joined his master and friend in a lively duet of pure sound. The snoring even drowned out the petulant buzzing of a hornet who was finding itself trapped at the windowpane.

Slocum had kept to his decision to sleep away from the McCormack house in town, but never stayed more than a single night in one place. And so he was a bit surprised when he heard someone approaching about an hour after he had bedded down. Instantly alert, he'd drawn his six-gun and moved away from his bedroll, which he left stuffed with a dummy he kept handy for just such an occasion. In the poor light of the early night, it looked as though he was indeed lying there in his bedding, whereas in reality he was several feet away, with his gun drawn and ready for action.

He could tell by the noise his visitor was making that it wasn't anybody bent on attack. And then, hearing a stifled curse, he knew who it was.

"Damn it, Slocum, where the hell are you?"

"You're late," he said, stepping out so that she could see him in the light of the moon.

Her voice was filled with surprise as she said, "You were expecting me?"

"Every night."

"I had to work out the time."

"Ben still away?" He was standing close to her now and smelling her perfume.

"I don't expect him back till tomorrow. He took Candy out to his camp on the North Fork."

"That's what I know," Slocum said. "Just wondered if he wasn't maybe back yet."

"Do we have to talk business?" she said. "Maybe I should've brought my teapot and some cups."

"Do we have to talk?" he countered. "Maybe you should have brought your nightdress."

"I brought everything we need, at least from this end of things," Honey Mellody said as she slid into his arms. "And that doesn't include a nightdress."

They were down on his bedroll now, pulling off each other's clothes as he drove his erection between her legs, which sprang apart with abandon, completely eager for his further thrust, now, as he mounted her and sank his shaft deep, high, and sure into her already soaking-wet passage.

Her squeal of delight in his ear urged him to press further, and now they began pumping, finding their rhythm together in the sureness of their coupling.

"I love it—I love it," she murmured, as their loins moved more quickly now, and, reaching around him, she dug her fingers into his pumping buttocks, while his erection probed hard all the way, rubbing its tip against the end of her vagina. Now their strokes quickened even more as he probed her, with each thrust more delightful than the last—until neither could hold it any longer, neither could stand even a second longer without release. And so, as their buttocks danced faster and faster and his organ grew longer, thicker, and harder, and Honey Mellody's soaking lips slipped faster and faster along his shaft, she almost screamed in her ecstasy and he had to put his hand over her mouth, but then released it as they came together in a rush of come that flowed out of her and down their thighs and on their bellies until there wasn't a single drop left.

Replete with their pleasure, they lay locked together, letting it all ebb. Presently he lifted himself away from her, though she still clung to him, and he lay beside her, her head nestling in the crook of his arm.

After a few moments they slept.

And they awakened as though they were one person. At the precise moment that he opened his eyes, the girl beside him opened hers. And as her hand dropped to his crotch, and he reached over to feel her nipple, his organ began to grow. In an instant it was at full attention, as were her nipples under the direction of his tickling tongue, his sucking lips, interspersed with little bites that drove her to an ecstasy bordering on madness.

"I want it sidesaddle this time," she whispered in his ear.

He didn't answer, only turned her on her side and slipped into her wet bush.

Presently he shifted his position, bringing her limber leg around and up and over his head so that he was lying on his side behind her.

"God, you did all that without taking your cock out," she marveled.

"And without missing a stroke either," Slocum said proudly.

"Slocum . . ."

"Yes."

"Let's fuck all night."

They did.

9

For a while then there was a lull, or so it appeared. Even so, Slocum knew he couldn't afford to let down on his vigilance. Big Ben was still only able to offer limited help, though he kept trying to do more, insisting that he was fully recovered. But he had his women to battle with on that. Plus Slocum, who came flat out and told him that unless he was one hundred percent well then he was more liability than help. This summation did not improve the McCormack temper, and his anger was taken out mostly on his wife, who bore it nobly.

Slocum, on the other hand, was fully earning his pay. He rode the stages as passenger, as shotgun, as driver. And he set traps for Dillingham's road agents. It was exhausting work: he couldn't be everywhere at once, nor could he take time off to be nowhere and simply do nothing for a spell, which in times of extended heavy action can also be necessary.

But the line was holding its own. The stages were getting through. Men had been shot at, three drivers and a guard had been wounded, and a guard had been killed. Slocum himself had miraculously escaped bullets thus far. And he knew that Dillingham's men were especially targeting him. The lull therefore was welcome, but at the same time it wasn't something he could count on. There could be no slackening off, and he told the men so.

Ben meanwhile had bought fresh horses, a dozen head to be exact, making fine teams, plus a half-dozen good saddle horses. Slocum was riding the buckskin McCormack had given him, besides a blue roan as a second mount. And he kept fresh saddle horses at the stage stations while he drove the coaches or rode shotgun.

"I think we've got 'em going," Big Ben said one evening as they sat having a drink at the big brick house at the edge of town. "They've been taking lead too, you know."

"That's for sure," Slocum agreed. "But you can't figure we've got 'em on the run. That Dillingham is no dummy. He may just be trying to tip us into thinking they're pulling back. Then they could really hit us, should we slacken off."

"I'll be riding the noon stage south tomorrow," Ben said suddenly. "I'm sick of settin' here. I'm in good shape, and I've had it out with Candy."

"I think we'd best double our men in the next few days," Slocum said.

"The men need a rest," argued McCormack. "But if you want to, if you say so," he added, "then it's all right with me."

"And I don't think you should be riding any stage yet. You're making a big mistake."

"I've decided that's what I'm going to do," Big Ben McCormack said.

And Slocum knew there was no arguing with the man. It was his stage line, after all, and it was his life he was laying on the line. Slocum said nothing. But he wondered again about the sense in whipping a dead horse. The stage lines were done for. Not long ago they had ribboned the country, but now it was only a matter of time, and a short time at that, before there wouldn't be a one left.

And still, he felt for a man like McCormack. The man had been one of the builders of the West. No question about it. Ben McCormack was a legend. While Slocum had simply agreed to take on the job of ramroding the line through. He had no doubt that he'd done the right thing. A man on the order of Ben McCormack needed siding. They were rare, those men. The Dillinghams, on the other hand, were not nearly rare enough.

Thing was, it had come at a time when he was truly on the loose. As a rule, he didn't take on jobs that were going to eat up so much of his time. But at the same time there was that gorgeous Honey Mellody, and that damned good-looking Jilly Barney. Yes, that Jilly Barney. By God, he was thinking, he'd better look her up. It was long overdue. Sure, she'd turned him down on having dinner, but she hadn't turned him down flat. It was high time he had another try at that girl. He owed it to himself to relax, to stretch himself, to enjoy the sweet after struggling with the bitter.

All the same, he remembered that there was something else that was overdue. There was the question of Sheriff Swede Byrner. Surely by now the man was up and about.

The door to the sheriff's office was closed, locked, and there was obviously nobody inside. Slocum wondered if

Hobe Winchy was still on as a deputy. Did the sheriff know what a crook he was carrying on the payroll? More than likely he did. Having been a lawman himself, Slocum knew how tough it was to get good deputies, men who were able and also willing to risk their lives for very small pay. In many cases, the minions of the law and the road agents, hoodlums, and slick gunmen were interchangeable. Henry Plummer was a notable example—or had been until he was caught and hanged by the Montana vigilantes. But there were others who played both sides of the law, just like Plummer, who had been sheriff of a territory bigger than some states and at the same time ran the road agents around the gold mines at Alder Gulch.

As he rode out of town now Slocum wondered if Byrner was one of these, or maybe just his deputy was playing both sides. Hell, no doubt Byrner, like so many others, had to take what he could get.

Slocum had thought he would take a short ride out of town just to get a change of scene. He needed to think. He knew that his men were tired, tired too of getting shot at, even though Big Ben paid them well. But that couldn't go on forever. Yet Ben had told him the government was going to have a hearing on the proposed railroad anytime now. It was because of this news that he had told McCormack not to let down, that the lull wasn't because the Dillingham forces were taking it easy now, or were about to give up. For it was clear to Slocum that Dillingham was probably girding himself and his men for a really big, even final, drive.

It was a very warm day, with soft, still air, as it is high in the mountains, while the hot light of the noonday sun on the prairie land reminded Slocum of the tawny color of a mountain lion he had shot a couple of years ago.

He had just come into sight of a low butte down by the

river when he heard the pistol shot. It came from somewhere close to the butte, and it was followed by another.
He immediately realized that it had to be somebody target
shooting. Lifting his reins slightly he kicked the buckskin
into a quick canter.

As he got closer to the butte and the river he began to
quarter back and forth, mindful of cover just in case it was
some kind of trap. Then he heard another gun shooting in
the same way. So it had to be two people, or possibly the
same person using two guns. But somehow, judging from
the spacing of the shots and the tempo of the shooting, he
knew it had to be two. And he remembered the attempted
dry gulching near Horse Gap.

Seeing a stand of aspen off to his right, he headed for it;
and cutting around to the other side, where he was sure he
wouldn't be seen by the shooters at the butte, he brought
the buckskin down to a fast walk as he closed in.

He took his time, drawing rein, listening, then moving
forward again. He had loosened his .44 for a quick draw if
necessary, and checked the Winchester in its scabbard.

Nothing happened. He rode closer until he was in full
view of the backs of a man and a girl, obviously somebody
quite young. They were shooting at bottles. Some were on
the ground; others were hanging from strings attached to
the branch of a cottonwood tree.

"You got to shoot like you're pointing with your finger,"
the man was saying. And he drew his gun slowly from its
holster and pointed toward one of the bottles. And pulled
the trigger. The bottle shattered.

"You going to try for the string?" the girl asked. And
before the man could answer she must have felt something
for she turned and saw Slocum and the buckskin.

Her surprise was certainly genuine, Slocum realized, as
he recognized her. But her companion remained looking at

the target, though it was obvious to Slocum that he knew he was there.

Slocum watched while the man raised his gun and pulled the trigger.

"You hit it! You hit it!" the girl cried. "You hit the string!"

Slowly the man lowered his arm and dropped the gun back into its holster. "You have a heap of practicing to do," he said.

Then he turned, and Slocum saw the brass star on his dark hickory shirt.

"Slocum." The voice was husky, declarative with authority.

Slocum touched the brim of his hat. "Sheriff." And he stepped down from the buckskin horse.

"Been wantin' to have a word with you," Swede Byrner said.

"Likewise." Slocum had in the meantime nodded to the young girl whom he had met previously when trying to visit the sheriff. "Glad to see your dad's better and up and about," he said amiably.

"Me too." She smiled, and the smile broke into a freckled grin. "Were you watching the target shooting?"

"I saw some of it."

"I'm not so good. But my dad's teaching me."

"I am not teaching you!" The voice was still husky, but now flecked with irritation. "I've just been showing you what you do *not* know about handling a firearm. Damn it! Young lady, you need some sense knocked into you, by jingo!" He turned to face Slocum head-on. "Wants to hire on as my deputy! Can you handle that? Jumping God and Jehosaphat!" He wheeled back on the girl, who was smiling pleasantly at Slocum and smoothing the sleeves of her silk shirt. "Now get the hosses. We got to git back to town!"

As she turned to go, his further words leapt at her. "Hurry up now! We ain't got all day to be lolligaggin' round this here!"

"Glad to see you're feeling better," Slocum said, and there was no sarcasm in his words. He meant it. "That's a fine young lady you've got there, Sheriff."

"An' I expect to keep her that way!" snapped back Swede Byrner. "Can you beat that! Wants to start packing a hogleg and accompanying me on my rounds and like. Get that! Boy! I seen it all now, by God!"

Fuming, the sheriff drew his six-gun from its well-worn holster and reloaded. Now he was calmer, though it was obvious to Slocum how much he'd been enjoying himself. The sheriff cocked an eye at him from beneath the brim of his battered Stetson hat. "Like I said, I want to have a word with you."

"And like I said—me too."

"Can't talk in front of the girl. Meet me at my office."

"Good enough. When's it suit you?"

"Make it after supper. Anytime after sundown is better, matter of fact. I'll be making my rounds, but you can catch up with me, or better wait in front of the office. She'll be locked if I ain't there."

He watched the sheriff walking slowly toward the girl, who was bringing their horses. Something familiar about him. But he couldn't place it. The face? No, not the face; that was too obvious anyway. The way he canted his head? Maybe. But who? Somebody...

Slocum had ground-hitched the buckskin close in to the steep side of the butte, and now he walked over and checked the cinch, then took the reins in his left hand, reached up, and with the same hand grabbed a fistful of long black mane, stepped into the stirrup, and swung up and over, all in one lithe movement. Once up, he spat casually over the horse's withers, then squinted at the sun, which was closing down on the horizon.

He let the two Byrners get a good start, and then he kicked the buckskin into a light canter. Buck responded like he'd known Slocum all his life. By golly, Slocum was thinking, that McCormack sure knew horseflesh. Well, he had to. Without the best in horseflesh his whole stagecoach enterprise would have folded long ago.

On the flat ground he let Buck right out, and they raced toward the distant foothills. Then he worked him into a weaving run, then brought him up short, kicked him into a fast go-again, slowed down, and worked him in the way of cutting out cattle. The buckskin responded right on the trigger. When he finally drew up for a rest, for both himself and Buck, Slocum valued Big Ben McCormack the more.

He sat the lion-colored pony with the black mane and tail and looked into the tinting sky as evening began to come. He could feel the new coolness of the coming night on his hands and face. It was good. It was good to get away from the town, the saloons, the honky-tonk noise and the crazy people. Maybe it was one thing the land was for—the prairie and the mountains—for a man to get away to.

He had wrapped his reins lightly around his saddle horn and had taken one foot out of his stirrup, and now he took out a quirly and lighted it. He felt good. Presently, he adjusted his Stetson hat at a different angle, stepped his foot back into its stirrup, then unwrapped his reins and kicked Buck into a canter.

Yes, he felt good. Damn good. But for the life of him he

still couldn't think who it was Sheriff Swede Byrner reminded him of.

"This time it's myself asking if you're looking for the doctor, miss."

Slocum had spotted her coming out of her father's office and locking the door behind her. She had just taken her key out of the lock when he spoke.

He found the surprise on her face a new delight. And this impression intensified when she smiled at him.

"Well, you've got me there," she said.

"I just reserved a table over at the Boston House," he said. "Expecting to run into you and that you would join me."

Her laughter was a further joy, and he felt something stirring deep inside him.

"Mr. Slocum, I—well I'm afraid I must again turn down your invitation. But another time." And she looked at him directly then. "If you will be patient with me. Things are . . . well, not very easy right now."

And without waiting for him to answer, she turned and walked off down the street.

Slocum watched her until she disappeared from sight, and then he crossed over to see if the sheriff had returned to his office. But the door was still locked, and there was no light inside.

It was early, and since he'd made the decision to move back into the East-West House, he decided it might be a good time to check in. By now he was fairly sure that Dillingham's men realized he'd been camping out and had possibly figured out his whereabouts. And while in one way he would have greater freedom outside in the event of trouble, in another way it was better to be in the hotel, where there were people around. And so he rode the buckskin out to where he had thrown his bedroll and picked up his warbag and bedding and rode back to the dilapidated hotel.

A half hour later he had transferred himself into a room at the East-West. The sour-looking, booze-and-onion-smelling gentleman at the desk had once again received him with the gravity of a gravedigger, asking once more whether he wanted a room "with" or "without."

"I'll bring my own 'with,'" Slocum said, hoping to raise a laugh or at least a smile. But he failed.

It was nighttime by the time he went down Main Street again to the sheriff's office. And he was pleased to see a light coming through the shaded windows.

A bark greeted Slocum's approach to the door, even before he tried the handle and knocked.

The door was opened by the sheriff. He was accompanied by Tip, the shepherd dog who sniffed at the newcomer's boots, then walked over to a favorite corner of the room and lay down.

"Where you throwin' yer duffle?" Swede Byrner asked as he shut the door behind Slocum.

"The East-West."

"Thought you might be stayin' with McCormack, but then I heard you was campin'."

"Figured a change might be good."

"Change is always good," Swede said. "Especially when things are happening."

He had sat down at his desk, and Slocum brought over an upended wooden crate and sat facing him. He took out a quirly and lighted it, his eyes on the sheriff, who was looking for something in his pile of papers.

"You maybe looking for that dodger on me?"

"I was." At that moment his hand pulled out the wanted

notice from halfway through the pile he'd been digging into. "Says you're a wanted man."

"That's what your deputy told me."

"He try to shake you down?"

"He tried."

"That's what I heard, though I guessed it anyways." Swede Byrner's eyes dropped again to the dodger. Then he tossed it down. "I reckon you've seen it."

"Yup."

"Who do you figure put it out?"

"Could be the Cattlemen's Association, but I'm inclined to think it was Dillingham. Of course, for all I know he could also be connected with the Cheyenne boys."

"Anyhow, I see you cut Hobe down to size. And a good thing. Though it won't do any good. Ever noticed? A fresh apple will get rotten, but the rotten apple never gets un-rotten. Funny, huh?"

The pale blue eyes of the sheriff were almost smiling, Slocum thought.

"You think you know me from somewhere, don't you, Slocum."

"You got a sharp eye, Sheriff."

"Have to in my business." He turned his head and spat in the general direction of a cuspidor that was resting by the potbellied stove in the middle of the room. His aim wasn't quite perfect. "What did you want to see me about?"

"What did you want to see *me* about, Sheriff?" Slocum said, coming right back at him. He had never believed much in letting the law get the upper hand unless maybe the talk was backed by a weapon and a man who knew how to use it. The sheriff of Hardins Crossing had both his hands on top of his desk.

A thin smile seemed to touch the sheriff's mouth, and

quickly vanished. "I already settled that," he said. And he tapped the dodger with his forefinger. Then he added, "That there, and I wanted to check the cut of your rig close up."

Slocum liked the way the man handled himself. There was not much wasted about the sheriff. Unlike many men, he seemed to move and speak as was necessary and no more. Like himself, Slocum knew. He always appreciated a man who knew how to handle his own strengths and weaknesses.

"I heard Ben McCormack got my name from you. That's how come he wrote me. That right?"

"I dunno if that's why he wrote, but I did recommend you when I heard he needed someone to ramrod his stage line after he got stove up from that bronc."

"How come?"

For a moment when the sheriff didn't say anything, Slocum began to think he just wasn't going to answer.

Then Byrner said, "I think I'll just hold on to them cards for a spell. They won't help the game any at this point."

He stood up, and the dog rose and came over, his tail wagging slowly, while his nose touched his master's trouser leg. Swede had taken off his hat and put it back on again, a little closer to his forehead. Then he canted his head and squinted at John Slocum.

"Good enough," Slocum said. He had also risen to his feet and started to turn toward the door. Yes, something familiar.

Suddenly Swede Byrner reached up and pulled at the lobe of his ear. "Just keep your nose clean, Slocum, and you'll be just fine with the law in Hardins Crossing."

"That's what I aim to do, Sheriff."

The sheriff stayed standing behind his desk as Slocum

walked to the door, opened it, stepped out onto the board-walk, and closed the door behind him.

Funny, he was thinking as he started along the street; funny how a simple gesture gave a man away. He still didn't know why Swede had recommended him to Big Ben McCormack, but that could wait. The important thing was he had seen Swede Byrner pull his earlobe—just like his brother Eddie Mulligan used to do.

The next morning Slocum walked down to the McCormack Overland office to see if Ben had possibly changed his mind about riding shotgun with Jed Prouty, one of his best drivers. But he already knew the answer. Ben was there in full force, giving orders right and left, supervising every-thing, and all the time pulling on one of his famous cigars. Slocum suddenly found himself wondering if the big ty-coon smoked in bed.

"Slocum, by God!" The voice boomed like a cannon across the street as Ben spotted him. "Come to see me off, huh? I wish you were coming along. No, I don't, you'd get in the way." And his remark was punctuated with a tre-mendous laugh as he looked around at the crowd who had gathered.

It was noon, and while the arrivals and departures of the stage were old stuff in Hardins, the event always drew a crowd.

Slocum stood to one side watching the proceedings, identifying himself with the spectators, in an effort to see the event from a different angle than his usual one. What had been forgotten? Had everything been taken care of? And so on.

He stood watching as Jed Prouty, the driver, came up from the stables with the empty stage and six fresh, eager horses. The teams were matched, and Slocum knew how Big Ben took pride in this.

Slocum watched the crowd as the crowd watched the strongbox being lifted into the leather-enclosed boot beneath the driver's seat. Then the mail sacks were stowed into the boot around the strongbox. And finally two men ·carried out the passengers' baggage and loaded it into the box at the rear of the stage. Some pieces that wouldn't fit were lashed on top, behind the driver. This gentleman remained in his seat, chewing rapidly on his fresh cut of tobacco, not deigning to offer a hand to the menials who were loading his coach.

Finally the passengers began to board. Of these there were a half dozen. The clerk who sold tickets inside the office came out then and helped three ladies to seats inside the coach. Then the men were allowed to board. At the last moment a man came running down the street, waving his arms and calling for the coach to wait. The clerk took his money, handed him a ticket, and threw his thumb toward the top of the coach. Since the inside was completely filled, the last passenger would ride on top with the baggage. As he scrambled aboard and the crowd cheered his successful effort, he started to lose his pants, and this brought the onlookers near to hysterics with laughter.

Slocum nodded to Big Ben McCormack, who was packing a brace of six-shooters at his belt and carrying a shotgun, as he swung casually up to sit beside the driver. Yet Slocum's quick eye caught the slight hesitancy in McCormack as his foot almost slipped on the wheel hub as he swung up.

The crowd had grown, and now it suddenly came charging to life as the driver uncoiled his whip, let it dangle for a moment clear of the coach, and then cracked it right between the ears of the lead team. With one leap the six horses took off. The coach sagged back the full length of its cradle springs and then shot forward as though fired from a catapult. The man on top was nearly thrown off but managed to grab on to something or other that saved him. The passengers inside the coach were thrown into each other's arms. The watching crowd roared with delight.

But John Slocum, walking down the slight grade toward the office, was wondering who the man was who had come running to catch the coach at the last minute. In any case, the man had retrieved his pants—to the cheers of the crowd of watchers. And Slocum was glad for that. He was suddenly aware that there was somebody at his side.

"By Harry, it's not everybody who can avert disaster at the eleventh hour like that and with the crowd cheering him on," said the rumbling voice of T. Wellington Throneberry. "That fellow can die happy now." And he chortled immensely at his sage observation.

He had braced Dillingham, but he knew the man hadn't slackened his efforts to break the McCormack stage line as a result of that meeting. He knew that things had to get settled soon or his own men—that is, McCormack's drivers, guards, and other employees of his company—would run down. He had fully realized that a man of Dillingham's reputation wouldn't be backed down easily. Face-to-face maybe, but not in the long term. Dillingham had strength in depth, that was absolutely clear. But Slocum had wanted to shake him, had wanted Dillingham to realize that although Ben McCormack was not fully in the picture, Dillingham still had a force to deal with. And Slocum was satisfied that he had gotten his point across. He had wanted to force the other man's hand.

He had just reached the part of town where the Boston House was situated when he saw Jilly Barney. She was coming out of a small store that sold cloth goods, and he immediately turned his steps in her direction. But before he'd even traveled two feet, he saw Quince Dillingham appear behind her, so he moved over to the side of the street, where he could not easily be seen, and waited.

She was evidently surprised to see Dillingham. Slocum had the feeling that the man had been waiting for her to appear; that maybe he'd even been following her. He wondered if it was Dillingham she had been planning to marry. Something in the man's stance and gestures told him it had to be.

The scene lasted only minutes. Evidently Dillingham was angry, but Slocum could see the girl was not cowed. She didn't raise her voice, or at least he couldn't hear her, but he could hear Dillingham. Not his actual words, but the sound, the anger he was getting across.

Suddenly Slocum saw Jilly Barney's face, white, set in pain and resolve as she turned and walked swiftly away. Dillingham started to follow, but apparently decided not to. But from the back Slocum could see the hardness of his shoulders, the thrust of his anger in his neck. The man was clenching his fists as he started across the street.

Slocum had sent three of his best men to follow after the stage, plus another three to deploy themselves at the stage stops where horses were changed and the passengers could rest and get a decent meal. Yet he still didn't feel easy. He had thought to go along himself—not with Ben, actually, for the big man would have been furious and would have refused—but to follow the coach. Yet he realized that would have been foolish, for he was definitely needed here, having, as it were, for the moment switched jobs with McCormack. In fact, it was a nice change.

At the sight of a prospector and his burro picking his way up Main Street his thoughts turned to the mine out by

Stark Canyon, the last of the mines in the area that was operative. It had occurred to him recently that Dillingham might be pulling something in that direction, and so he decided to pay a visit to the sheriff. He was lucky. Sheriff Swede Byrner was in his office, and he was alone, save for his dog, who was lying by the window gnawing on a bone.

"No," Swede had said, "that mine don't pay much. Besides, Dillingham's bought up a helluva lot of real estate hereabouts. He's got a pretty full plate. Anything doing with the mine wouldn't match the railroad deal he hopes to pull off." The sheriff leaned down by the cuspidor that was next to his desk and, placing his thumb alongside one nostril, he blew, then switched to the other nostril and did the same; both movements were executed with neat proficiency, Slocum noted. Relieved, Swede sat up and said, "Shouldn't you be out on McCormack's run? You got a day off or somethin'?" His eyes were filled with humor at the thought of anybody having a day off, it seemed. "I see Ben took your job away from you," he went on.

Then from the back room his daughter walked in, and Slocum realized why the lawman was in such good spirits. Sally Byrner had the kind of life in her young body, in her smile, in her gestures, and in the way she moved that could enliven anything. In fact, Tip dropped his bone and came over with his tail wagging and licked the side of her shoe.

"Well, miss, you in here to straighten up your dad's desk?" Slocum asked with a grin.

"She better know better than to touch anything on this here," her father warned. "Now you skedaddle on home, Sal. Me and Mr. Slocum here have got things to talk over."

She came up behind him then and slid her hands down around his neck and hugged him. "I'm going to be practicing my fast draw. Lightning Sal, that's what the eastern magazines will call me."

"You even touch that handgun again without me bein' there and I'll paddle you, so help me!" Swede wasn't fooling, and they both saw that.

Putting a pretty insincere sulk expression on her face, the girl retreated, waving at the door to Slocum, but now with a big smile for him.

Slocum was chuckling as the door closed.

"You got more trouble there than me and Ben have with Dillingham," Slocum said.

Swede didn't respond to Slocum's jocular tone. Instead he sat looking down at his hand that was lying on a pile of papers on the desk.

Without looking up he said, "How about signing on as a deputy, Slocum?"

Nothing could have surprised Slocum more, and he almost said so. Instead he grinned at the sheriff. "Even with that wanted notice out on me?"

"You know that's a fake."

"I sure do. I was funning," Slocum said.

"But I'm serious," Byrner insisted. "I just can't get men wanting to side the law, to take the responsibility. Figgered you might."

"I have to turn you down. I got a job. Besides, how would it look if I was your deputy while at the same time working with McCormack?"

"It would look damn funny. But it might not look so funny if I end up working this town with no help."

"Can't you get some one from Cheyenne?"

"I've asked and asked." He spread his hands wide apart, shrugging. "Nothing. I shouldn't have asked you. I had to try everything."

He sniffed, leaned down, and blew his nose again, and cussed. "Slocum," he said, straightening up. "You knew Eddie Mulligan."

"I sure did know your brother."

Swede nodded, a wry look on his lined face. "Then you know I used to ride with Eddie and his boys."

"Or was it Eddie used to ride with you?" Slocum added.

"Right. That's right." Swede nodded. "But I quit. Got shot up and just made it, and I quit when I met up with Sal's mother."

"How long have you been with the law?"

"About six years, give or take."

"They know down in Cheyenne?"

Swede lifted his hands again, shrugging. "Dunno. But you know how it is, you do your job and that's what the law wants—I mean like out in this country. Elsewhere, who knows? Maybe you got to be a preacher man."

"But are you square with the law?" Slocum asked.

"I don't owe the law a thing. But you know I changed my name on account of people get ideas."

"Does Ben know who you are?"

"Ben knows. It's why I told him to get hold of you when he started having his trouble. Ben helped me—he helped me a lot when Sarah was sick, and then when she was dying. I didn't have any money. Nothing. I couldn't have made it, and I had Sal to take care of. I owe Ben McCormack a whole helluva lot."

He sniffed again, but didn't bend over to blow his nose. "I was out of line askin' you about taking on as deputy. It's better you stay like you are."

"I think that's right," Slocum said. "But what about Dillingham? Does he know?"

"I think he does now."

"What do you mean 'now'?" Slocum asked, catching something in the other's voice.

"I mean Manny O'Hagen's in town."

Slocum said nothing.

"You know him?" Swede asked.

"Only by name."

"Manny used to ride with me an' Eddie and the boys." Swede Byrner was leaning forward on the desk, with his right forearm outstretched, leaning on it a little. He was looking down at his right hand, moving the fingers a little.

"See, I can shoot pretty good at a target, like when I can get set and take my time. But when it comes to a draw..." He didn't finish; he was still looking down at his fingers.

"What's he doing in town?" Slocum asked, though he already knew.

"Dillingham."

Slocum nodded. "That figures."

He felt Swede Byrner's eyes on him. "I figure it was O'Hagen drygulched Eddie. Can't prove it. But I'm going to, one way or the other."

"And then?" But Slocum knew the answer to that one too.

"I'll kill him."

"What about Sal? What about your daughter?"

Swede Byrner didn't answer. He stood up and walked to the gun cabinet on the far side of the room. He unlocked it and took out a cut-down shotgun. Then he closed the cabinet and locked it. Crossing to his desk, he opened a drawer and took out a box of shells for the shotgun.

Slocum was watching him closely.

"Time for my rounds," Swede said. "I'm taking this extra along—in case."

They left the office together. The evening star was in the western sky as they came out the door.

10

Slocum had been leery about Big Ben's taking the noon coach southeast; not only about his traveling that long journey so soon after his accident, but his actually taking on the job of riding shotgun.

McCormack had of course scoffed at the notion that he was taking a risk, pointing out that there had been a definite lull in Dillingham's activities, and that anyway he could handle anything that came along. Anything! There was no arguing with the man, as Slocum saw.

He had thought of sending riders along to precede the coach and some others to follow it. And he'd told the idea to Ben, feeling that he'd better know beforehand in case something went wrong and signals got crossed. Ben wouldn't have it. There was nothing to do but let him go.

Slocum, now working closer with the office at the stage depot in Hardins, was well aware of the fact that Lead

City's Gore, Ajax & Thunderclap Mine was almost doubling its shipments south on the McCormack line, and that Hardins' lone mining operation was suddenly booming, adding more to the problem of shipping by stage.

There could be no question but that Quince Dillingham had to be aware of these facts. Why then had he slackened off his harassment of the stage line? And was it only coincidence that the two mines that shipped by stage to Cheyenne had suddenly issued figures that indicated close to a doubling of their output? Why at this particular time, when Washington was on the verge of deciding whether or not to renew McCormack's contract, or to grant permission for new track to be laid which would wipe out one of the last stage routes in the West?

Slocum knew that Ben was well aware of all the implications that were suddenly rushing to a climax demanding action. They had discussed it all forward and backward the night before he'd taken his shotgun down to the depot and announced that he was riding with Jed Prouty.

But Slocum also realized that Dillingham would have enough sense not to go too far with things. It was one thing to hold up some stages, or to do a little sabotaging around the depots, wrecking harness, stealing supplies, and in one case before Slocum's arrival on the scene, knocking down a wooden bridge—events that were seemingly isolated, not related to any single plan aimed against the company. That is, nothing evident to the law as such. Accidents, due to random thieves or the forces of nature, such as a huge boulder dislodged during a thunderstorm and rolling down a long slope to block the roadway of the stage. For Dillingham had to be mindful of public opinion and the law. At the same time, Slocum knew very well that the present lull was only temporary, that it actually heralded a big offensive. But how? How and where would Dillingham and his gunslingers attack? And what role would Manny O'Hagen play? Had Dillingham hired him to run his gunmen, in the light of the failures of Print LeJeune and Hobe Winchy?

It seemed obvious that O'Hagen was playing a central role in the Dillingham game. It also seemed obvious that Manny O'Hagen was interested in counting coup at Slocum's expense.

He checked into the passenger who had arrived late for the stage and satisfied himself that he had nothing to do with the Dillingham forces, that he was simply what he had appeared to be—a young man who had come close to missing the stage south, not to mention his pants. But as a result of his suspicions Slocum realized how sharp he had become in regard to the whole situation, and he was glad of that. For somehow he knew that something was going to happen pretty soon. Very soon. Of this he was convinced.

The aged clerk saw him the moment he walked into the East-West, and without any gesture or even a word, Slocum knew the man wanted to see him about something. He strode quickly across the empty lobby and found the man's wet-looking eyes staring intently with his news.

"Had a visitor," he said, lowering his voice almost too far for Slocum to hear him.

"Female, I reckon, from the way you're talking," Slocum said.

The clerk's liquid eyes appeared to be loose in his head, or Slocum wondered if maybe it was the bad lighting. In any case, the man nodded. "Sent her off, and she left this note for you."

"Why didn't you tell her to wait?" Slocum said, sticking his tongue in his cheek so the oldster would know he was funning.

But the clerk took it straight. "Couldn't read your mind from that far a distance, sir."

Slocum chuckled at that, happy at the way the old man had come back at him.

"Good enough," he said and opened the note and read: "Can I see you for advice about something?" It was unsigned, but he knew it could only be Jilly Barney. The handwriting was clear, the lines were straight. It had to be her. The only other could have been Honey Mellody, who would have chosen to come and see him rather than send a note; or possibly Candy McCormack, who he couldn't see resorting to this method of reaching him.

He was feeling pretty good as he approached the doctor's office, hoping she was there. And there was always the question of surprise, for even before he had touched the doorknob, it turned and the door opened from the inside.

"Mr. Slocum, have you come to see me or my father."

"Where shall we go?" he said.

"There's a place where we can have some coffee if that would be all right. Say, in the Boston House, the restaurant." She paused a moment. "I think it's better if I meet you there. Will that be all right? It's better if we're not seen together."

"Meet you there," Slocum said. "But right now, you'd better let me in. There's someone across the street mighty interested in our conversation. Let me in like I was calling as a patient."

She stepped back quickly and allowed him to enter.

"My father's out on a call," she said as she closed the door after him. "Maybe we could talk here. Then if he gets back we can leave and meet at the Boston House."

"Fine." He was happy to be in her presence, finding her even more attractive than before. At the same time he could see that she was upset over something, even bordering on distraught.

"I'm sorry to bother you," she began, seating herself opposite him. "By the way, if somebody should come in, I'll be examining your shoulder."

Slocum nodded. "So what's the problem? You're not bothering me."

She looked down at her hands, and he noticed that there was still no wedding or engagement ring on her finger. He was relieved. Her black hair was hanging down, and now she swept it back and threw her head back and looked directly at him out of those fabulous blue eyes.

"As you see, I'm not getting married. It—it was a hasty thing, not something I really wanted to do."

"Mind if I ask who the man was?"

"I don't mind. I don't mind at all. It was Quince Dillingham." She raised her head a little more and seemed to straighten her shoulders. "I guess I'd like to tell you the whole thing. I mean, my reasons."

Slocum said nothing.

"Dad—my father . . ." and she glanced toward the door, then went on. "Dad had some difficulty some years ago. Not in Hardins. East of here. And somehow, I don't know how he ever did, somehow Quince Dillingham knew about it, or found out about it. Somehow."

She stopped and bit her lower lip. Slocum saw that she was fighting tears.

"I get it," he said gently.

"He wanted our land, Dad's land not far out of town on Betty Creek. And—he also wanted me."

"That's understandable—for anybody to want you, I mean," replied Slocum.

She wiped a tear that had started to roll down her cheek, and now took hold of herself. "But I couldn't go through with it. I—I just couldn't." She suddenly looked at him directly, her big eyes beseeching. "Please, Mr. Slocum. Dad doesn't know anything about this end of it. He has agreed to let Dillingham have the land—they've agreed on a small price, something ridiculously low. But—but my part . . . I can't. I can't!"

She looked down, fighting her tears, her hands gripped into fists on her knees.

"Are you worried he'll take it out on your father in some way?" Slocum said.

"I don't know. No, I can't think that. He got the land he wanted. And—and you know, I never encouraged him. He just seemed to look upon me as some kind of object that he ought to have. Damn!" She dabbed at her eyes with a small handkerchief that she had taken from her bosom.

Slocum was thinking what a marvelous bosom she must have, judging from its contours, which were pressing against her silk shirt.

"Excuse my language," she said, and he smiled.

"You're excused. How about some coffee if that interested party is gone?"

"I do want to. But I'm upset now. I do want to. But maybe when I'm not so upset. I don't want Dad to know about this."

"He won't know about it from me," Slocum said. "And I can wait. But now, how can I be of help to you?"

"I don't know. Maybe I just had to talk to—to someone who's friendly and seems to understand. Is that all right?" She seemed suddenly alarmed. "I'm not trying to use you; at least I don't think so. But I am a little afraid, I guess. I've heard some rather nasty things about Quince Dillingham."

"I'm sure they're all true," Slocum said. "I'll do whatever I can."

"Maybe, just to talk to a bit. I think that's the best—"

"Has your father signed any papers yet on his property?"

"I don't believe so."

"See if you can get him to wait. I don't know what can be done. As far as you're concerned, all you have to do is say no. With your father and the land, maybe I could look into it."

"Oh, would you? I mean, I don't know if Dad would agree, and I don't want to use up a lot of your time."

"At least I won't expect you to marry me," Slocum said with a grin, and the remark, and perhaps especially the way he said it, made her laugh.

"Thank you," she said. "Thank you for making me feel better."

She had just dried her eyes when there was a knock at the door and one of Doc Barney's patients came in.

"I'll see you soon," Slocum said. "Meanwhile, I'll be turning all this over."

She saw him to the door and, as he was leaving, touched his arm gently. He liked that.

As he walked away he saw no sign of the man he'd noticed earlier across the street. But his arm where she had touched him felt good.

Hobe Winchy's walleye itched, and so he scratched it. Then he ran his forefinger along the length of the scar on his face.

"Boss, I want Slocum." And he looked over at Print LeJeune, who was seated in the other chair facing Dillingham's desk.

"Details," Quince Dillingham said. "But don't worry. I'll decide who is going to do what to whom." He reached over to the silver cigar box on his desk, opened it, and took out one cigar, not offering the box to the two men. Leaning back, he bit the little bullet out of the end of the long Havana and then, striking a wooden lucifer along the underside of his desktop, he lighted up.

"You will each have plenty to handle. And I want one thing clear: you will do exactly as you are told. There will be no deciding on either of your parts as to what or how. If and when I tell one or both of you to kill Slocum, then and only then will you do it. Do you understand me?"

"I do," Print LeJeune muttered.

"Yeah." Hobe Winchy's words came out as dully as Print's.

"Good. You both understand. You know the consequences of what happens to anybody who decides to run his own operation. Just remember Fernando."

They both remembered what had happened to the Mexican horse wrangler only too well.

Quince Dillingham allowed a moment of the memory of that disciplinary example to sink in.

"Then we will have no problem. You men will be ready with the dynamite at the Medicine Bow bridge, one of you on each side of the river with your men. You have the names." He leaned forward on his desk, taking a long pull at his cigar and releasing the blue smoke toward the ceiling of the room.

"Now then. I shall arrange a signal for you, and you will be told in plenty of time what it is. You will then simply follow the instructions I've given you."

"Blow the bridge and the coach, horses, and passengers and driver and guard," said Print, and he slapped his thigh in acknowledgment of the neatness of the plan.

"You will do what you are told, and I have not told you about blowing any coach and passengers into the river, you goddamned idiot!" Dillingham's anger was like cold steel as his eyes riveted LeJeune. "Do you want the whole territory coming after us like a lynch mob, for God sake! What the hell is the matter with you!"

Print had paled to an ashen white under the lash of Dillingham's words. And what upset him even more was to see the smug expression on his companion's face at his misfortune.

"And you can stop grinning like a goddamn hyena, Winchy!" snapped Dillingham. "If one of you—I say, one—fucks up on this operation, you both will pay for it. Is that understood? Do you understand me? Say it!"

"Yes, got'cha," said Hobe almost before Dillingham had finished speaking.

And Print's words were already overlapping him.

"That will be all." The voice from the other side of the big desk was as calm and cold as death.

Five minutes later, when Manny O'Hagen walked into Dillingham's office and sat down in an easy chair across the room, his employer of the moment indicated with his forefinger the silver cigar box.

Silently the tall man with the narrow shoulders rose and walked over to the desk. There was a smile on his face as he opened the silver box and took out a cigar and, picking up the matches on the desk, lighted it.

"Not bad." And he reached in and took two more cigars and put them in his pocket.

"Come closer so we can talk," Dillingham said. "We're getting down to the main event here."

Manny O'Hagen pushed one of the recently vacated chairs closer to the desk with his boot and sat down. "I saw your two boys leaving," he said. "They didn't look very happy."

"A touch of discipline was necessary," Dillingham said easily." He chuckled softly. "I should have said a threat."

"Keep the boys in line, huh?" O'Hagen looked at the ash forming on the end of his cigar. "What about the men, then?"

"I want you to take care of Slocum."

"That's exactly what I'm figuring on doing."

"What I'm saying is that those two, LeJeune and Winchy, are really wanting to square things with Slocum. I don't want them getting to him first."

"They won't."

"You've got to be sure, O'Hagen. See, if those two foul up my plan we could be in trouble. They could talk, is what I'm getting at."

"You want me to see to it that they don't talk?"

"Maybe afterwards."

"After? After Slocum?"

"After the whole plan is completed."

"You mean the bridge."

"The bridge blown, but nobody—I repeat—nobody hurt. I don't want the law down on me." He held up his hand as O'Hagen moved to speak. "I am still treating Swede Byrner, or Mulligan, as I always have. He's the sheriff, and just because he does have a past he will obey the law better—which is exactly what I want, without him turning it on me."

Manny O'Hagen said nothing to that, but kept his eyes moving around the room, aware that Dillingham was watching him closely.

"And, uh, O'Hagen, we must be careful therefore that nothing happens to Swede."

"I wouldn't harm even one of his fingernails," the narrow-shouldered man said.

"Well, then as soon as I get clearance on the decision in Washington we can go ahead. Should be any time now." And he stood up to signal that the meeting was ended.

Manny O'Hagen got very slowly to his feet, and this action was not lost upon his host.

Together they walked to the door.

"Good then, O'Hagen," Dillingham said, and refrained from patting the other man on the shoulder as he would have done with anyone else in his line of business after a well-understood meeting.

Instead he said once again, "Then we're clear on Byrner—that nothing happens to him. So that he can report to the law through the eyes of the law. Get it?"

"I wouldn't harm even one of his fingernails," Manny O'Hagen said, repeating himself word for word, tone for tone.

"Thing is, we have got to get some more men," Big Ben was saying to John Slocum.

"Fine. But how?"

"I know that by now Dillingham's got news that the agency passing on the proposition has set a deadline."

"I agree," Slocum said. "So we've got to keep a healthy line open till the seventeenth. That right? That the way it reads?"

"That's how she reads."

They were sitting in a back room at the One-And-Only Saloon and Gaming Parlor, having a drink, a sandwich, and a talk. Big Ben's ride as shotgun messenger on one of his own coaches had passed without incident, and he had returned full of vigor. It was just then that he received news from Washington that the committee that would grant or refuse permission for the continuation of his stage line would be voting within the next two weeks. This would of course affect the plans for the new railroad line east to St. Joe.

"All we got to do is keep the line open. But you see,

Slocum, that sonofabitch Dillingham has got to have someone on that committee."

"Because he knew enough to draw back for the past couple of weeks and leave us alone."

"That's what I mean. He's got to have inside information."

"And now with the news coming about the deadline he'll go all out," Slocum said, summing it up as though he was thinking the whole situation out loud. "That's why we need more men, I know. But we need to look at their weak spot. Let's face it, we can't get any more men."

He had been in the middle of his last sentence or two when there had come a knock at the door, which both of them had ignored. And now, just as he was finishing, the door opened and in walked T. Wellington Throneberry.

"Gentlemen, allow me to announce that you are not entirely without major support. You have me, yours truly, T. Wellington Throneberry himself in person!" And with a flourish he swept his hat from his head and held it in the crook of his arm, standing there as though posing for a photograph or an oil painting.

"You will pardon my interrupting you, but no one answered my knock. I am at your service!"

"Come in, come in," McCormack said.

"I already am in, Mr. McCormack. But if I may, I will sit down. Age, you know. It does creep up on one."

"You're not serious about offering yourself to me—us," McCormack said, his broad face wrinkled in disbelief.

"Mr. McCormack, let me put it this way: I am a man who has recently passed his three-score-and-ten, yet I retain the lithe mobility of my youth, not to mention intelligence, a quality the minions of the law might wish for. I assure you I can be an asset to your enterprise. As credentials, you might wish to contact Sheriff Swede Byrner, who, in point of fact, recommended that I present myself to you both, uh, in the capacity of a law-abiding citizen, a diligent, able-bodied man of talent, honor, and, uh, moral support."

"Holy shit," said Big Ben McCormack. He looked toward Slocum, who was standing, having risen from his chair to call the bartender for another beer.

"I say we take him," Slocum said as he opened the door and called out for another round. Returning, he said, "You like a drink, Mr. Throneberry?"

"Indeed I would. Uh, if you don't mind, gentlemen, I took the liberty of speaking to Harry, the bartender, on my way in, instructing him to bring me something if I stayed over five minutes in your company. I hope that was all right." And his eyes swept swiftly back and forth between the two men for confirmation.

Slocum couldn't help but laugh.

"I'll take him," Ben said with a heavy sigh. "Jesus! We are scraping the barrel."

"The best liquor is in the squeezin's, sir. Any man of substance, such as yourselves here, knows that. The top of the barrel is for the boys. Now then"—he looked up as Harry the bartender entered with three glasses of refreshment—"just what can I do for you gentlemen?"

"You know what's going on with Dillingham, do you?" McCormack asked. "I got a notion you do. Are you workin' for the railroad? Let's cut all the funnin'. What's your angle." And suddenly Big Ben was hard as a rock.

"You've been working for the sheriff, haven't you?" Slocum said.

The surprise on T. W.'s face was genuine. "How did you figure that, young man?"

"Seen you coming and going from his place. Who you reporting on?"

"That is a secret. But the sheriff did send me to you to see if you could use me. All funnin' aside," he added, looking reproachfully at Big Ben. "You can check with him."

"We'll check on you with Swede Byrner, no question," Slocum said. "Meanwhile, tell us what you know about Quince Dillingham. I mean, his moves, his likes and dislikes, everything."

T. W. beamed. "I see you are more than merely observant, Mr. Washington—excuse me, Mr. Slocum, sir—you can almost read minds, I do declare. Gentlemen, may I sit?"

It was a day and a half later that T. W., to use his own phrase, "earned his spurs" in the stagecoach-railroad battle. Ben McCormack had received news from Washington that the committee concerned with western transport was about to convene. This meant that there would be a decision forthcoming on the McCormack contract. It meant, as Slocum pointed out, that Dillingham would intensify his efforts to smash the coach line.

"You sure said it," agreed Big Ben as he sat in the Hardins stage depot with Slocum and T. W., who had just come in with news of his own.

"So what have you got?" Slocum asked T. W. after a moment of digesting the news about Washington. "You find out anything useful?"

"Don't know where it fits, gentlemen, but Mr. Dillingham, who was planning on marrying a certain young lady here in Hardins, appears to already have a wife in Denver. And before that another one in San Francisco."

"That's interesting," Slocum said, "but I don't think that can help us much. You agree, Ben?"

McCormack nodded. "That I do."

"Unless we were running a political campaign, or something like that where we would be concerned with someone's private life, I don't see how it can help. But try again, T. W. At least he's got his ear to the ground, eh, Ben?"

Big Ben chuckled at that but said nothing.

"You don't want to use it to twist the sonofabitch?" T. W. asked.

"Even if we did, it would take time," Slocum pointed out. "With the news that the committee in Washington is having at it right now, we've got to act fast, because sure as hell Dillingham will."

"I have more news," said T. W., undaunted by momentary failure.

"About Dillingham?"

"About Sheriff Swede Byrner. But let me first say it isn't anything against him. I am still working for the sheriff in whatever capacity I can. I told you why. What I am about to relate to you is something I discovered by the way, as it were. By accident."

"So what is it?"

"Swede was not shot up so badly in the fighting with those roisterers from the Circle Slash, who were mixed in with some of Dillingham's men."

"What do you mean?" McCormack asked. He had been tilting back in his chair, and now he let the chair drop forward onto its front legs, his eyes firm on T. W. Throneberry.

"I mean he did take some lead in that encounter, but not that much. A couple of flesh wounds, actually, and he killed two of the men and scared off the rest."

"So what are you saying?" Slocum demanded. "Come on, T. W."

"Swede was shot later, that same night, when he was sitting in the outhouse back of his office."

"Why didn't he tell us?" Slocum said.

"You weren't here to tell, and McCormack there was laid up. He mentioned it to me, just by the way, like everybody knew that already."

"Jesus H. Christ." This exclamation was followed by a low, wet whistle from Ben McCormack's pursed lips.

"Wait a minute," Slocum was saying. "You're saying that shooting, the outhouse thing, was an intentional effort to kill him, where before it was just a bunch of Circle Slash saddle drunks living it wild and he busted them?"

T. W. inclined his head gravely. "That is how I sum up the situation."

"But where does that leave Dillingham? We've been figuring he wanted Swede alive as a witness to himself going by the law on the up-and-up. With a suddenly dead sheriff Cheyenne would send marshals in here pronto. Dillingham isn't a fool."

T. W. raised his heavy white eyebrows, spread his hands apart, and shrugged, absolving himself of any responsibility in the affair.

Slocum took out a quirly but didn't light it right away. He held it in his fingers, turning it around slowly as he studied what T. W. Throneberry had brought.

"Likely Dillingham was trying to throw a scare into him," he said. "Wanted Swede to know he'd better toe the line. Wanted him to feel a little insecure. Maybe. Maybe he knows something about Byrner, and Byrner might be wondering if he does or doesn't."

"They could have killed him easy," Ben pointed out. "A sitting crapper. Easy as a watched Puritan finding his own ass in daytime."

"Right enough," Slocum agreed. "So that's why they didn't kill him."

"Why?" asked T. W., looking dumb.

"Like we just told you!" snapped McCormack.

"Course, course." T. W. cleared his throat of phlegm along with the slight misunderstanding. Uncle Obie had long ago taught him the value of the throat-clearing as a means to not say anything while still saying something.

Suddenly Slocum took out a lucifer and quickly lighted the quirly his fingers had been playing with.

"Well, I've got a question here. What do you figure was in those boxes that a couple of muleskinners were packing on a freighter wagon last night, heading toward Eagle Pass?"

"Who were they, do you know?" Ben McCormack asked.

"Never saw them before."

"Did you follow them?"

"Not right away."

"But what made you so suspicious?" Ben asked. "Nothing wrong with freight heading out of town. Happens all the time."

"I know. But when I asked one of them where they were heading he said Tenfork."

"That's the Ajax, at Tenfork."

"Right." Slocum took a drag on his quirly. "Only thing is they were headed in the opposite direction."

"Those jaspers are up to something!" exclaimed T. W., his pale eyes wide with excitement.

"They were heading in the direction of Eagle Pass." Slocum took another drag on his quirly. "I waited and followed them a ways, but then I noticed they had outriders so I laid off."

A sharp whistle broke from Big Ben McCormack.

"You're telling us that they were heading more or less in the direction of Eagle Pass, which leads on down to Cheyenne. In other words . . ." He paused, knitting his brow.

"In other words, they'll be going over that bridge across Butte River. Or," Slocum added, "stopping nearby."

Ben McCormack was looking at him curiously. "Dynamite?"

"That's what I'm thinking. Didn't you tell me they blew up a bridge some while earlier this year?"

McCormack was nodding. "The bridge at Eagle Pass is a pretty solid structure, but if they blow it we're in big trouble." McCormack was sitting up straight in his chair. "That's the one route across the Butte River. We'd lose a day having to go around."

"We'd lose our contract," Slocum said. "It means they know something."

"How so?"

"They're getting desperate. They know or maybe just strongly suspect that the committee's going to vote for a new stage franchise. They blow that bridge, we've got to go around by Wood Lodge." He had crossed to the map on the far wall on which the stage routes were marked in red.

"But they've got to blow it without anyone getting caught," Slocum continued, his eyes on the map. "And they're going to have to do it right away. I'll bet Dillingham knows we've got a big shipment going out from the mines, from Ajax."

"At the same time," put in McCormack, "they don't want to blow it too soon, so'd we find out about it and have time to go a different route."

T. W. had been silent during this exchange, sucking his teeth thoughtfully, pursing his lips, and gazing into the far corner of the ceiling. Then maybe he dozed off, for he jumped when Slocum spoke.

"I'm thinking of Swede Byrner in his outhouse."

Both men stared at him in amazement.

"You gone crazy, Slocum?" McCormack was wagging his big head from side to side, not believing what he had just heard. "Tell me what in hell Swede Byrner getting shot up in an outhouse has got to do with blowing Eagle Pass bridge to hell and gone with dynamite!"

"The way we figure it, Dillingham ordered his men to scare Byrner, or at least warn him. Not kill him. But it looks like they might have gotten a little too eager and like to *did* damn near kill him. What I'm saying is Dillingham thinks like a fox—he does something, lays on something, but he's always got something else going at the same time, is the way I see it. And I just smell something suspicious with Eagle Pass."

"You're thinking it's maybe a decoy."

"I'm only saying maybe."

"But he's going to have to hit someplace," suddenly put in T. W.

"Where do you think?" said Ben, who didn't like long talking and was getting impatient. "Up King Solomon's ass?"

"In the outhouse," T.W. said, the words seeming somehow to pop out of his mouth without his having sent them.

"Holy shit on a shingle!" McCormack roared, "What kind of the hell asshole talk is that!"

"It might not be the bridge at all, or anything with the coaches," Slocum said, ignoring McCormack's outburst, his eyes directly on T. W. "That's how I read you. It'll be something personal."

"That is precisely what I was getting at, Slocum. As the

old saying has it, great minds often see a thing at the very same moment."

"Let's cut the shit," snapped McCormack, his big body tight with impatience. "Where the hell are we?"

"Maybe with a shoot-out, and if so, it'll be a whole lot sooner than anything that would take place on the route."

"You mean he could send someone gunning for you or me?"

"Or me?" added T. W. pointing his long, thin forefinger toward himself, as even his nose paled at such a thought.

"Or maybe all of it," said Slocum, suddenly getting to his feet. "The bridge, a drygulching, the whole thing. Why not?"

"Where are you going, John?" It was the first time McCormack had called him by his first name.

"To take a look at the town. To get Swede Byrner ready, and then—since you hired me to ramrod this here outfit—then I want you to get a dozen men and meet me a half mile out of town on the south trail. In an hour."

"You gonna let me ride with you?"

Slocum stood at the door with his hand on the knob. "I wouldn't have it any otherwise," he said with a slow grin.

11

It was evening. Slocum had spent the day checking the stage route down as far as Eagle Pass and across the bridge to the south side of the Butte River. He was looking for likely places for an ambush, a rock fall, anyplace where dynamite might be used. He was sure that it had been dynamite in the wooden cases the wagon had been hauling the night he'd spoken to the man skinning the mule.

By nightfall he was satisfied that Eagle Pass Bridge was the logical place for Dillingham to strike. And in fact when he rode down to the north side of the bridge and met Ben McCormack and his men, he learned that they had found crates of dynamite hidden in a thick stand of cottonwoods and willows.

"But there was more than this on that wagon," he said, picking out one of the sticks and breaking it open to examine it.

At this point one of the men came riding across the bridge, followed by two more riders. "There's a stack of crates on the other side," the rider said.

"That'll take care of the wagonload, wouldn't you guess, Slocum?" Ben was studying the sky. "Looks to be clear tomorrow."

"I figure that would make the load. But why did they leave this here? It's hidden, but it isn't hidden the way you or me would hide it."

"You mean they want it to be found," T. W. said. He was still stiff from his long ride from town, and in sore need of a drink of whiskey, which nobody seemed to have on hand.

"That's sure a helluva note," T. W. continued.

"Lucky we found it now, then," Slocum replied.

"I'm talking about there being no whiskey to hand," T. W. said severely. "A hell of a way to run a posse of grown, earnest, hardworking men!"

At this point Ben McCormack reached into his saddlebag and brought forth a bottle.

"Praise the Lord!" T. W.'s milky blue eyes rose toward the deep sky overhead. "And bless you, Benjamin McCormack. In return I will serve you to the . . . to the, uh, hilt!"

"There's the route between Ajax and Hardins," McCormack suggested. "Can you think of any place there that might make an ambush? Any place they could use dynamite?"

Slocum shook his head. "I've been over that route already, what I did with the whole line when I hired on. There's no place there. Nothing."

"Then they're wanting us to be here, waiting for them to come and blow up the bridge."

"That's it," Slocum said. "And meanwhile back at the

stage depot . . ." He let the rest of the sentence hang but was already mounting the buckskin horse.

"Ben, we'll head for the Ajax and bring that shipment into town tonight. You send a couple of fast riders ahead who'll tell them to load up and get started. The shipment is due in Hardins tomorrow noon. But I want it there before dawn. Well before dawn. Can you ride with them to follow it up?"

"What the hell d'you mean can I ride with 'em!" And he was already stepping into his stirrup and swinging onto his big dun horse.

"We'll all meet at the depot. But let me repeat: the Ajax shipment has got to be at the depot before there's any light. Now send those fast riders ahead with the message, and then you follow up. Me and T. W. here will be scouting your back trail and flanks."

To his left Slocum heard Throneberry murmuring something or other. "Something the matter, T. W.?"

"Slocum, I am no longer a young man. I don't know about all this riding. I am getting on."

"You should have thought of that before you joined up."

And that was the full cup of sympathy that T. W. Throneberry was able to elicit from his stern companion.

It was evening when Slocum and T. W. reached Hardins. He had let McCormack and his men go on ahead, skirting the town to camp about halfway to the Ajax, at Singletree Creek. From there in the middle of the night they would go on to the mine, pick up the shipment, and return to Hardins before dawn. Slocum planned to keep on their back trail in case of any Dillingham riders being about. For the moment, though, he and T. W. would rest their horses in town, and Slocum would check the stage depot to see if anything special had come over the wire.

"You stay in town here while I'll be checking on any loose riders about on the way to Ajax," he said to T. W.

"I was planning to go with you, Slocum."

"Think you can keep up?"

"Don't be ridiculous!"

Slocum didn't argue the point. He liked the old man's spirit, and he did have a good head on his shoulders.

"Why didn't they set the dynamite to blow up the bridge?" Throneberry had asked as they reached the old roadbed at the edge of town.

"To keep us guessing, I reckon."

"And what if they take the gold shipment before it gets here? I mean, suppose they've got enough men to outshoot McCormack and his boys."

"They won't do that. See, Dillingham's game is to show that the stage can't handle its business."

"Then why not just blow up Eagle Pass bridge and be shut of it? What's all this outfoxing business for? Hell, he's got cards. Why don't he play 'em?"

"My friend, you're a gambler, and if you don't remember that the one cardinal weapon of the ace gambler is surprise then you don't deserve the title of master gambler. Am I right?"

T. W. had flushed as he realized the dumb way he'd set himself up. "You look to me to be pretty damn good at the cards yourself, Mr. Washington, sir!" And he accompanied his reference to their old joke with a chuckle.

"I play people, just like you do, T. W., not cards. Only fools play the cards."

"By the Lord Harry! You sound like my Uncle Obediah! Mr. Washington, you are indeed a man of divers parts! I take off my hat to you." And with a grand flourish he swept his huge Stetson hat from his head. The result was that his horse spooked and came close to unseating him.

"Careful, careful," Slocum cautioned as T. W. clung to his saddle horn. "We'll split up here," he went on, drawing rein. "See you before dawn at the depot. And stay sober!"

He had ridden McCormack's back trail, finding no sign of any other riders. It was late when he returned to Hardins. The lively part of town was going with everything it had; the rest of the populace slept. Riding along Main Street he saw that there was a light in Doc Barney's office, and on an impulse he drew rein, stepped down, and led the buckskin over to a hitching rail. Then he stepped onto the boardwalk and in a moment was knocking at the door.

The shade was down on the front window, and now somebody pulled back a corner of it to see who was there. Then the door was unlocked and Slocum found himself confronting Jilly Barney.

"Hope I'm not disturbing you," he said. "But I saw your light on."

"Do come in," she said, stepping back.

As he entered she closed the door behind him. When they faced each other in the light of the coal oil lamps he saw that she was tense and pale.

"Something wrong?" he asked.

"No, I don't believe so." And she tried a smile, but it didn't work. "Only that I feel there's something going on in town. Dad felt the same. He was here and just left. Sorry you missed him."

"I wanted to see you, not him. But what do you mean, something going on?"

"There were a lot of men riding in a couple of hours ago. And I don't know if it means anything to you, but I saw Quince Dillingham talking to some of them. It was quite by accident. I happened to be out because Dad sent me for something that he had at home and needed for a patient."

"Tell your dad to stay off the street tomorrow morning," Slocum said. "And that goes for yourself, too."

"There'll be trouble?"

"Plenty of it." He took his hat off. "Can I sit down a minute?"

"Oh, of course, how rude of me. I'm sorry."

"You've actually helped me. I mean that what I only suspected your words tell me is true. The showdown will be here in town."

"Showdown?"

"Some gunfighting. That's why you and your father stay inside."

She had paled even more, he noticed.

"We'll be needed if people get hurt."

"Yes, but wait till they do get hurt," he said. He stood up. "I think I'll leave you. Or can I walk you home?"

"You think it won't be safe?"

"I think it's all right, but I wanted the pleasure of walking you home."

Suddenly she smiled, and he felt something stop inside himself. She was beautiful.

"I would like that pleasure too," she said.

As they left he said, "I'm afraid I'll have to keep some of my attention on the street. Can't be helped."

She didn't say anything to that, but fell in step beside him, and in only a few minutes they were at the door of her home.

"I'll say good-night now," she said. And she looked around. "I should be cautious too. Jealous suitors are not something I enjoy, especially when they've only just been rejected."

Then there came a moment when they looked at each

other. Slocum had his eyes on her full lips, then looked into her eyes. The next thing he knew he was kissing her. Her lips were soft, and cool and warm at the same time.

"Good-night," she said, drawing away after a moment.

"Stay inside tomorrow, remember. Both of you."

"Thank you."

In the next moment she had entered her house.

So it was going to be here, in Hardins. Of that he was now certain as he awakened to the sound of the horses approaching outside the depot.

It was still night, but he could feel the stirring of the coming dawn. He'd slept only a short while.

"Any trouble?" he asked Ben McCormack as he opened the door to let the men enter.

"Nothing. How about here?"

"A lot of men came into town."

"O'Hagen?"

"Very likely." He waited while McCormack directed the men as to where to put the shipment from the mine.

"You sure it's going to be here?" Big Ben asked when everything was settled and they were having coffee.

"It'll be a gunfight. That's the way I see it. O'Hagen is a pistoleer, right? And he'll want to go up against me. To put it simply—they knock me off, then they can get you, is how they figure. And then they'll just take over everything."

"They must see by now that they can't get us on the stage route. They've been trying long enough," McCormack said.

"They see they've got to work fast, and if they bugger up another stage job, they're through. This way, they hope they can bust us, right now."

"Where do you want me and the men?" Ben said.

Slocum had seated himself at the desk, and now he picked up a sheet of paper and a pencil and drew a map of Main Street.

"Here on the roof, in the alley, inside the East-West. I want men having breakfast—that is, pretending to have it—in these places." Quickly he marked the places that he wished covered.

"But where will I be?" Ben said.

"You cover me, but you've got to keep out of sight. See, I don't know where O'Hagen or the others will pick their fight, so you'll have to be on the move."

"What if O'Hagen doesn't pick a fight?" McCormack asked. "That likely?"

"It sure is, and I've thought of it. I'll see that he does."

McCormack chuckled. "Good enough."

"Where do you want me?" T. W. asked, moving in closer on the conversation.

"You stay out of it."

"I say, that's not very sporting of you. I want to be a part of things. In the thick of it, by jingo! I helped lead up to this climax, and now I don't expect to be separated from the action."

But Slocum had no time for long-windedness, and he said quickly, "You watch me, understand? I'll be their target, and you'll be my extra eyes."

"Which is what I'll be doing, Slocum," said Sheriff Swede Byrner as he walked into the room.

"How did you get in?" McCormack wanted to know.

"I happen to be the sheriff of this here town, case you forgot, mister!"

"Good to see you, Sheriff." Slocum grinned at the angry man of the law.

"I ought to arrest the bunch of you. Only thing is, all the damn paperwork. Howsomever, I will be watching the action—closely—and I'll be enforcing the law as need be. This thing's gone too far now for me to stop it single-handed, though if I was twenty years younger it'd sure as hell be a different story."

"News sure travels fast, Sheriff," Slocum said.

"And what the hell is he doing here!" glared Swede Byrner, as he spotted T. W. standing behind somebody at the rear of the room.

"I'm helping the cause of law and order, Sheriff, and fulfilling my duty in regard to yourself."

"Then thanks a heap for letting me know all this was going on," snarled the man of the law.

"Didn't want to speak too previous to you, Sheriff Byrner—like before things were ready."

"Bullshit, Throneberry. You mind me now. You watch your step, by God!"

"I will, sir. I'll watch my step!"

"Get out of here, all of you," Slocum said, standing up suddenly. "Take those spots on the map I drew, those of you who Ben picks." He turned back to Swede Byrner. "Sheriff, I aim to abide by the law, but I do believe that at least one man is gunning for me, and maybe three or even four. What do you say to that?"

"I say you're behind the eight ball, Slocum, but I'll just move over so's we both of us have enough room." Dropping his eyelid in a slow wink, the sheriff of Hardins Crossing said, "I need a deputy, Slocum."

"Not me. I got to work this my way, Sheriff."

"I wasn't askin' you," Byrner snapped. "But I am tellin' this man." And he nodded his head in the direction of T. Wellington Throneberry, whose face went ash white.

"Come on, T. W., haul your ass up to my office. I'm gonna pin a star on you and hand you a cut-down Greener twelve-gauge."

"I—I'm afraid I don't know that weapon, Sheriff." The words came stammering out of the suddenly very small-looking Throneberry.

"All you got to do is point it and pull the trigger, Deputy. Now let's go."

The day broke on the town in total silence. Without any warning, light suddenly was there filling the great sky. Before the sun had risen people were stirring, cocks crowed, dogs barked, here and there a horse nickered. It was just slightly cool on T. W. Throneberry's elbows as he rolled up his sleeves to wash his face in a bowl of cold water.

Sheriff Swede Byrner had stepped behind his house to urinate more or less out of sight, while the dog Tip followed suit. From within the house came the rich odor of Sally Byrner's coffee and baking-powder biscuits.

Doc Barney was stropping his straight razor, checking its edge with his thumb until he cut himself slightly and he swore. His daughter Jilly was looking at herself in her bedroom mirror, wondering if John Slocum had noticed the suggestion of a wen—which she considered a disfigurement—behind her ear. Honey Mellody was still asleep. Candy McCormack was standing by the window of the big brick house watching her husband walking away from the front door and heading toward the stage depot.

At the livery, Slocum checked his saddle gear and the buckskin horse and gave a silver dollar to the old hostler as an extra. Buck was saddled and bridled and ready to go when needed.

"Expectin' action, are you?" Cracker John, the aged hostler said, then let fly in the direction of a scurrying pack rat but didn't even come close.

"Might be," Slocum said, keeping his eye on the oldster, for he'd caught something in the man's tone.

"Got trouble with the pack rats in this place," Cracker John said, and raised his eyes toward the loft.

In that same instant Slocum dove to his left as the shot rang out and the bullet smashed into the floor where he had been standing a half second ago.

He was on his back and rolling, his Colt in his hand as he came up in one of the empty stalls. The buckskin whickered loud as Slocum snapped a shot at a sudden movement he caught up in the hay loft. His aim was true. The man dropped like a sack of wheat onto the floor of the livery, and the buckskin started to spook.

Meanwhile, Cracker John had found cover. Slocum could hear him near the little room at the far end of the livery.

Now, keeping under cover, Slocum worked his way to the tack room and Cracker John.

"There's two of them," the hostler whispered. "You got one to go."

They waited, and then all at once Slocum heard the man drop out of the hayloft onto the ground outside the livery. In a trice he was at the door and had brought down the second man.

"Turk Garton and Wild Bill Jorgeson," Cracker John said, in the tone of a coroner doing his business.

"Nice to meet the boys," Slocum said. "Take care of Buck there, Cracker John."

The shots had brought no one out to the street, though he spotted some of McCormack's men on a couple of roof-tops and alleys. But there was no sign of any of the Dillingham gunmen, other than those two former gunhawks lying inside and outside Cracker John's livery.

It seemed more quiet than necessary. There was no sound of life—no dog barking, or door slamming, not even a horse nickering. In fact, there was not a single horse at any hitching rail. He looked again at the rooftops and alleys and saw something.

At that same moment he heard Print LeJeune's harsh voice in the soft morning air.

"Slocum! Hold it right there. We've got McCormack, and you drop your gun right there!"

Slocum took another look at the rooftops and saw that one of the men Ben had assigned was covered by another man out of sight. That had been the glint of gunmetal that he had seen. But where was Swede Byrner? Where was T. W.? Then he heard Big Ben.

"That's right, Slocum. They got me. You were right, I should've taken more time to heal, goddamn it! But listen, John. Get the sons of—"

Slocum heard the thud of something hard hitting bone, and Big Ben McCormack was cut off.

"Slocum! You got three seconds to drop your gun or McCormack is dead!" It was Print LeJeune again.

But before Slocum could make a move still another voice cut into the tableau.

"Leave him his gun. I want to see if he knows how to use it."

Slocum had never seen Manny O'Hagen, but he knew him the moment he stepped out from the alleyway. The man with the narrow shoulders and the brace of tied-down six-guns. And black eyes in an almost chalk-white face.

It was the perfect setup, Slocum could see. Manny O'Hagen in front of him, and Print LeJeune and probably Hobe Winchy for good measure behind and to the side.

"Slocum, I'm gonna show you who the fastest gun is."

"I already know that, Manny boy."

And Slocum was on the ground as three shots rang out, cutting the air above him. He had the Colt out and shot Print LeJeune right through the heart as he stood on the boardwalk in front of Bremer's General Store, and then fired his second bullet into the walleye of Hobe Winchy.

The bullets from Winchy, LeJeune, and O'Hagen had swept harmlessly over him as he dove to the ground. His third antagonist had however hit the dirt, which Slocum only discovered after he had disposed of the two bushwhackers who had set him up for a back-shooting.

Manny O'Hagen was flat on the ground and struggling to rise. It was only when Slocum heard Swede Byrner's voice cutting into the street that he realized what had happened.

"That was for Eddie, you sonofabitch!" Then the sheriff raised his voice so that it rocketed off the houses lining the street. "The rest of you men are under arrest. Throw down your guns! McCormack, your men can collect 'em!"

Big Ben McCormack gave the order right now, as the street began to fill with his men taking Quince Dillingham's hired gunmen into custody.

Slocum suddenly spotted Sally Byrner on the boardwalk across from him, watching her father. And that moment almost cost him his life. He was standing close to Swede Byrner when something went through him like a hot chill. In one streaking second he had whirled, drawn his six-gun as a shout went up from the onlookers, and shot Manny O'Hagen right between the eyes.

As T. Wellington Throneberry was to tell it all over the town and throughout a large part of the West in years to come, no one had ever seen a man move that fast. Nobody! First Slocum had wiped out LeJeune and Winchy, and then swifter than a striking rattler he'd drawn on O'Hagen while the gunman still had his weapon in his hand and was faking dying—and killed him.

* * *

"Well," said Big Ben McCormack, "let's drink to the end of Quince Dillingham."

"He's really left town?" Slocum asked.

"That's the reliable report. And all thanks to you, my friend. Boy, I sure buggered it up there for you this morning."

"No, you didn't."

"The old body just wasn't able to do what I'd always told it. Sonofabitch!"

"Actually, you built a good setup for me. And for Swede. He got his evens with O'Hagen, and his daughter can't tell him he actually killed the man. She's hot for him to quit guns. And I agree with her. He's an old codger, but a damn good man. I'd never have been able to handle those three alone."

"I think you could've," Big Ben said. "And I'll drink to that. I should say, I know you could have. On account of you damn well did!"

At which point there was a knock at the brick house door and T. Wellington Throneberry appeared.

"Gentlemen, Mr. Dillingham has left town, and the marshal's office at Cheyenne is in hot pursuit. Meanwhile, yours truly has been exonerated. All—all has been forgiven!"

"Congratulations!"

"You are facing a free man."

"What are you aiming to do now, T. W.?" Big Ben asked.

"I shall return to an earlier love—the scrivener's trade, and shall document for posterity—and for cash too, let me add—the fantastic exploits of one John Slocum. The story should make a million."

Slocum's words came then like chips of ice. "You do that and I promise you—and I have a witness here—that there will be an extra writing on the subject about how the said Slocum shot, killed, and hung the author out to dry. Put that in your cigar and smoke it—Terwilliger!"

T. W. looked as though he was about to be violently sick. Finally controlling himself, he gasped, and at last managed to say, his voice muted with agony, "How—how did you ever hear that name?"

"Never mind, Terwill, old boy," Slocum said, imitating him heavily. "I'll keep my mouth shut, and you do the same."

"Done!"

And they shook on it.

Later, in his room at the East-West, Slocum took hold of Jilly Barney's hand, only he didn't shake it. She had asked him as they lay side by side in his bed if she might take hold of his penis. In reply he simply took her hand and wrapped it around his rigid member.

"Tell you an old saying, young girl," he said.

"What?" she whispered, breathing the word in his ear.

"Actions speak louder than words."

JAKE LOGAN

____ 0-425-09342-5	RAWHIDE JUSTICE	$2.50
____ 0-425-09395-6	SLOCUM AND THE INDIAN GHOST	$2.50
____ 0-425-09567-3	SLOCUM AND THE ARIZONA COWBOYS	$2.75
____ 0-425-09647-5	SIXGUN CEMETERY	$2.75
____ 0-425-09896-6	HELL'S FURY	$2.75
____ 0-425-10016-2	HIGH, WIDE AND DEADLY	$2.75
____ 0-425-09783-8	SLOCUM AND THE WILD STALLION CHASE	$2.75
____ 0-425-10116-9	SLOCUM AND THE LAREDO SHOWDOWN	$2.75
____ 0-425-10188-6	SLOCUM AND THE CLAIM JUMPERS	$2.75
____ 0-425-10419-2	SLOCUM AND THE CHEROKEE MANHUNT	$2.75
____ 0-425-10347-1	SIXGUNS AT SILVERADO	$2.75
____ 0-425-10489-3	SLOCUM AND THE EL PASO BLOOD FUED	$2.75
____ 0-425-10555-5	SLOCUM AND THE BLOOD RAGE	$2.75
____ 0-425-10635-7	SLOCUM AND THE CRACKER CREEK KILLERS	$2.75
____ 0-425-10701-9	SLOCUM AND THE RED RIVER RENEGADES	$2.75
____ 0-425-10758-2	SLOCUM AND THE GUNFIGHTER'S GREED	$2.75
____ 0-425-10850-3	SIXGUN LAW	$2.75
____ 0-425-10889-9	SLOCUM AND THE ARIZONA KIDNAPPERS	$2.95
____ 0-425-10935-6	SLOCUM AND THE HANGING TREE	$2.95
____ 0-425-10984-4	SLOCUM AND THE ABILENE SWINDLE	$2.95
____ 0-425-11233-0	BLOOD AT THE CROSSING	$2.95
____ 0-425-11056-7	SLOCUM AND THE BUFFALO HUNTERS (On sale October '88)	$2.95
____ 0-425-11194-6	SLOCUM AND THE PREACHER'S DAUGHTER (On sale November '88)	$2.95

Please send the titles I've checked above. Mail orders to:

BERKLEY PUBLISHING GROUP
390 Murray Hill Pkwy., Dept. B
East Rutherford, NJ 07073

NAME_____

ADDRESS_____

CITY_____

STATE_____ZIP_____

Please allow 6 weeks for delivery.
Prices are subject to change without notice.

POSTAGE & HANDLING:
$1.00 for one book, $.25 for each
additional. Do not exceed $3.50.

BOOK TOTAL	$_____
SHIPPING & HANDLING	$_____
APPLICABLE SALES TAX (CA, NJ, NY, PA)	$_____
TOTAL AMOUNT DUE PAYABLE IN US FUNDS. (No cash orders accepted.)	$_____

LONGARM

Explore the exciting Old West with
one of the men who made it wild'